Eurydice Priest and the Wild Hunt

Copyright © 2024 Adam Schubert

All rights reserved. No part of this book may be reproduced or transmitted in any form or by any means, electronic or mechanical, including photocopying, recording or by any information storage and retrieval system without permission in writing from the publisher.

Violent Rooster Press—Belleville, WI
ISBN: 979-8-9919617-0-7
eBook ISBN: 979-8-3305-6463-7
Library of Congress Control Number: 2024924360
Title: *Eurydice Priest and the Wild Hunt*
Author: Adam Schubert
Digital distribution | 2024
Paperback | 2024

This is a work of fiction. The characters, names, incidents, places, and dialogue are products of the author's imagination, and are not to be construed as real.

Published in the United States by New Book Authors Publishing

Eurydice Priest and the Wild Hunt

Adam Schubert

Brigadier Price and the Wild Hunt

John Lambert

Dedication

This is for my mom
And my little guy Ollie
Sometimes dreams come true

Prologue

Morning sunlight filtered through trees and rolled through valley mists. A circle of caravans huddled around a communal bonfire. From the mess tent, the smells of coffee, tea and burnt cedar greeting nests of birds and small rodents. Purple morning twilight gave way to crisp golden dawn.

Three sisters, triplets, rose to the morning bird calls. Stretching, their joints cracked from the too-small, too-hard mattresses in their camper. Strange dreams disturbed their slumber that night. Not that this was unusual. Strange dreams defined their lives, awake and asleep. But these dreams bore special importance.

"It's happening again," one sister grunted as they sat, their minds cloudy. Sunlight of perception seeped into their awareness. "Another one is about to expire."

"From what direction will it come?" This sister sat on the northernmost cot. Vintage monitors fired to life one by one, illuminating the small room with malachite light.

The third sister, crouched on the eastern bunk, yawned and smacked her lips. "It comes from the east with the dawn." She sniffed. "Either we need a bath or this termination will be harsher than the last."

"It's both," the second sister said. "I can taste myself." She stuck her tongue out and grimaced.

"How will it go this time?" The first sister asked. She had coffee going on a small, battered hot plate. "Is it coming by land, sea or air?"

"It comes from without," the second sister said. "Not from the depths like the Great Old Ones, nor from the sky like the Xenos." She passed a jar of sweet honey to her sister and licked the residue from her fingers. "This will be from In Between. It will have the precision of a tornado and the sweep of a hurricane."

"It will shake the earth with many feet, crushing mountains and filling valleys," the third sister chimed in.

"What will draw it out?" The first sister asked, pouring their coffee, mixing in the honey.

"Hubris," the second sister replied.

"Pride," the third sister said.

"A woman," they said in unison.

"The usual," the first sister calculated, passing cups of coffee to her sisters.

All three grabbed towels and trudged to the narrow river behind their camp. Already awake and moving, their honor guard gave salute and greetings over their own breakfast fires. The aroma of bacon and eggs clouded the women's minds with hunger as they bathed.

Strange dreams. Stranger than their last client. Fog and shadows smudged the details, but they could see their client, plain as day.

Back in their caravan, they dressed per their tradition. The three sisters put on matching pinstripe suits, worn and shiny from years of love and use. The inside lining was a deep crimson. Cufflinks and studs of tarnished silver and polished onyx glinted in the dim light.

The eldest sister inquired, "Are we prepared?" As she spoke, she donned a helmet adorned with optical components that sparkled in the light. Her two siblings responded with a nod, then proceeded to put on their own helmets. They lowered themselves onto a plush, overstuffed sofa situated in the center of the room.

"Draw the cards," the first sister said. "I can't take the anticipation."

The third sister reached into a battered sandalwood box, removing a deck of cards, battered, bent and shiny with age. She licked her thumb and the cards fanned out in a blur. Fan, bridge, shuffle. Fan, bridge, shuffle. She spread the deck out on their coffee table. "Draw three," she commanded to the first sister.

"The fool, the king and the tower, laid upside-down," she said.

"Draw three," the third sister told her second sister.

"The hanged man, judgment and the boatman, also laid upside down."

The third sister drew her three cards. "The page of pentacles, the lovers (upside down) and," she flipped her final card, "the death card."

"Same old cliche," they sang at once.

The first sister pursed her lips, dissatisfied with the fan of cards before them. She scooped the cards up and reshuffled. "One more draw," she directed. "I'll take the first card, then you draw," she pointed to her sister in the middle. "Then you," she told her third sister. She drew a card. "The Hierophant," she said.

"The hermit," the second sister said.

"Death again," the third sister flicked the card to the pile from her fingertips. "But upside down, this time."

"The game begins once more," the second sister said as their minds blended together. "The last one was so messy," she grimaced.

"Let's hope our client stays to play the whole game," the third sister said as time and space unwound in spiraling fractals.

"*Quidquid, erit*[1]," all three said as one, and fell silent. The eternal game picked up once more.

---

[1] Whatever, it will be

Chapter 1

Gracie Caer threw her rucksack to the ground in a cloud of dust and wrinkled her nose. The atmosphere could curdle milk, she thought with more than enough generosity. Her journeys across the Novum Imperium Romanum were over. Dust, death, leather, shit-all these aromas she'd grown used to. Her intimate knowledge of nomadic odors from the past three (or was it four weeks?) paled compared to the chemical fumes and industrial miasma that belched over all. Mile-high smokestacks sprouted somewhere deep within the city, raking the sky.

The city-state squatted on an isthmus between two vast inland seas of pure mercury. The city did what it could to filter its atmosphere, but the dead earth suffered the consequences. The only trees and grasses that grew in that landscape sat stunted and poisonous. Legends speculated the seas once held millions of gallons of fresh water, but few could be sure. Three cycles of dark ages scrubbed that detail from the history books. If there was water, someone replaced it, but details of that lost alchemy failed to surface. The metallic fluid rippled and shifted under its unusual currents.

Everything within Kalkaska's steel walls stood monotonous against sullen skies. Gracie felt the city's cicada hum days before she saw its minarets looming above the horizon. The walls supported a massive particle accelerator, the source of the city's power. Maglocks the size of tractor trailers at the end of pistons broader than subway tubes kept the city safe. Oil dripped from every surface, flowed through the streets and misted in the air. Everything shone like a metal rainbow.

But she was here, and her search was almost complete. Her task, or punishment, was threefold. She would travel to

Kalkaska, and locate the hermetic Adeptus Degory Priest. That done, she would identify the whereabouts of his current bodyguard, and take his place. *Facilius dictum quam factum*[2].

If rumors were true, Priest did not relish uninvited guests. The Central City organized itself according to ancient virtues of law and efficiency. Kalkaska had its own method and madness. Millions swarmed the streets and walkways in a tangled web that was more hive than city. Streets branched and radiated in three dimensions around a cryptic central hub. Rather than traveling home, the people here lived in dorms provided by their work blocks. The perpetual throbbing rumble was their nightly lullaby. She felt a million unseen eyes upon her, examining her, dissecting her. Forbidden Kalkaska, Kalkaska the Feared, Kalkaska the Hellcity. Kalkaska had an earned reputation for feeding on outsiders.

Gracie reviewed her notes, hoping for some clues to track her predecessor down. She needed to find a bar or pub to feed her hunger for food and info. Her throat burned for a drink and a tortured rainbow of neon signs beckoned her away from the caravan depot.

***

In the city's core, past a ring of dense trees that circles the city's center, sits Priest Labs. Its utilitarian slab dominated the landscape. Professor Degory Priest lounged on a beach chair under a big umbrella in the sun-scorched parking lot outside the lab's glass foyer. He wore dark sunglasses over bloodshot eyes, his lab coat hung limp over his frail frame, hinting of his lack of nourishment and exercise. A flying vehicle, its massive propeller-wings still spinning, crouched before him on the broad tarmac. Before long, three figures emerged and advanced toward him with a purpose he failed to like.

"What are you going on about," he asked the three officials, representatives of the Central Houses. Two men and a woman

---

[2] Easier said than done

in military uniform stood before him doing their best to appear intimidating. "I've been busy. I can't keep up with every memo you send my way."

"We've been trying to reach you for the last two weeks," the man on the left said. "You haven't been sending your reports and," he sniffed, "your minder has been out of contact for the last three."

"I have been busy," Priest said slowly, "and I can't be bothered to babysit my babysitter if he's going to go wandering."

"You've been given explicit instructions to adhere to your assignments," the woman in the middle said. "No more side projects. Clean air, water and dirt within two years. These were your priorities," she said. "Everything else is irrelevant."

Priest cracked his thin, wiry neck, looking past the trio of interlopers. They had snipers, drones circling above and an assault squad on call. He could see the sweat at their temples and the nervous tension in their postures. "I think you're being short sighted about this," he retorted.

"Nonetheless," this time, it was the man to the right of the woman. He had dark stains under his armpits already. "These orders come from the top and we expect you to follow them to the letter." He tossed a fat manilla envelope into Priest's lap the same way one threw out a soiled diaper. "Your new minder is inbound as we speak. We will be expecting reports from her and we expect you to fall in line."

A slow smile crossed Priest's lips. The three officials moved back a step in unison, but Priest kept smiling. "Fine," he said, standing. He let the envelope with its unread contents fall to the concrete, scattering with the hot, dry wind. "Send your errand-girl and I'll put her to good use," he paused, relishing their mixed reactions to his suggestion. "Rather, I'll set her to work, right away," he chuckled. He returned to the cool darkness of his labs, his mind already buzzing with plans. If his plans lined up with his tormentors' plans, he need only divert his attention to a more entertaining task. Let the minder come. Let the guard become the prisoner.

Priest smiled a quiet smile as he navigated the pristine labyrinth to his quarters. Playtime was about to begin.

***

Dense crowds pressed her tight as she fought her way into the spider's web. Workers in drab uniforms stomped in an endless cycle between their homes and jobs. Despite previous surveillance, Kalkaska's fluid nature and vibrant culture made her maps irrelevant. The city's intense EM field made her compass useless in the web of alleys and culverts. Factory dorms and company stores competed with brothels and drug dens. Each fork and branch led to more branches. She pulled a small can of ultraviolet reflecting paint, noting her lefts and rights.

Litter drifted from the higher walkways like bitter snow. Before it could land, recycling crews snapped it up for the molecular breakdown tanks. No matter how much rubbish got scooped up, the perpetual oil slick flowed over everything.

The smell of alcohol cut through the oily brine in the air, leading her to the first welcome sight since arrival. Burning Fumes operated out of a dwelling no deeper than a closet, boasting an aura unique. The city air was fresh next to the odor that boiled out of the cramped saloon tasting of body odor and stale beer. An antique jukebox played corrupted bootleg downloads from a broken speaker. Gracie took a deep breath of poisonous air and slipped into the bar.

"What'll it be?" The bartender's red beard filled his face. An implant behind his ear twinkled with lights. Pinups, faded from the sun, hung at odd angles behind him.

Gracie held up two coins, disks of cherry gold metal, between her fingers. "What'll this get me," she asked, the ghost of a smile crossing her lips. "I'm quite thirsty."

The bartender looked from the coins and back to Gracie. "Local currency only, Miss," he spat, "If I took foreign cash, I would go broke in a vault full of worthless change." Gracie held the bartender's eyes in hers. "Please, miss," he said, voice less hostile this time, "no trouble. That's all I ask."

"Two things," she drawled, handing him a pair of thick gold washers, "a drink in a clean glass and some information. *In vino, veritas*[3]."

The bartender barked a nervous laugh. "That's three things. I can pour you a drink," sweat shone bright on his forehead, "but the price of information has gone up." He shook his head. "And third, if you want a clean glass," he spat into a glass and wiped it with a filthy rag, "you're going to have to go elsewhere."

"I'll buy the bottle," she dropped another washer. "I came a long way and I'm dead thirsty." She dropped her bag to the floor and leaned on the bar.

His eyes dropped and he reached under the bar. "For a stranger on a long path who knows what she wants, we've got synthetic tequila." He looked around with squinted eyes, then fished a vial on a chain from inside his shirt. A stunted, evil looking leach twisted around in predatory figure-eights. He cupped his hand around the vial and the leach glowed with bioluminescent blues and yellows. "For another two, I can add one of these to it," he waggled his eyebrows at her, his smile daring her.

She looked at the worm in the vial, squinting at its patterns. "What is it," she asked.

"Not sure," the barman held the vial to the light, shaking it a little. "The guy I bought it from said it's good. Do you want it or not?"

She nodded, holding his eyes with hers, and slapped more washers on the bar. The worm writhed as it dissolved with fizzling bubbles into a hallucinogenic cloud. Gracie Caer smiled and swirled it, gazing into the streaked cup.

"I'm looking for someone," she said, drinking a mouthful, savoring the burn. It felt like velvet on heroin.

---

[3] Truth in wine

"For love or revenge," he asked, leaning on the bar. "From the looks of you," his teeth were a dentist's nightmare, "my guess is it could go either way."

"No," she said, "this is business and they say he's a homebody. I can't find his place." She lit a cigarillo, her eyes chips of ice as she looked at the bartender.

"What's your business with him?" His hand never betrayed him.

"That's private," she clucked her tongue. "I need to find this man," she pulled a worn notebook from her jacket and read the name with sharp vowels. "Adeptus Degory Priest." She laid down a chemphoto, a true image no less, of a scarecrow of a man, wrapped in secondhand labwear. The photo was a representation of Priest taken from a telecamera. Radiation from the battery powering his prosthetic arm created distortions in the picture. "My sources say he's an overdue library book that needs returning." She breathed deep, "in fact," she said, "this entire city has gone dark. There's a pattern of lost cities, strung out in a chain," she smacked her forehead and laughed. "It's quite the quandary."

The bartender stared at the picture brow furrowed into a tangle of thick hair and deep folds. Dull apathy clapped down hard over a brief flash of recognition. "He doesn't exist," he said, voice deadpan. "Go home."

"Rumors say otherwise." She tapped another coin on the bar. "Can't go home until I've found him." She treated him to a practiced smile that recommended he save himself from the world of pain and play along.

"I- I can't say for certain," he stuttered. His eyes darted around as if a chorus of voices all shouted vindictive threats down at him. "There's nobody like that here. I'm telling you, go home." Gracie's eyes narrowed to dangerous slits but never faltered. Her jaw tightened and she reached down to her hip, unsnapping a hunting knife attached to her belt. She was getting to the end of asking with nice words. Was this a sign that her tolerance for strong drink was starting to fade? Was it the glowing flatworm whispering in her ear? She pulled a pamphlet for Priest labs from her pocket instead. "How do I get here," she asked, her voice a silk razor blade. She even arched an eyebrow, hoping he would read interest in the gesture.

That broke through a mental firewall. "The labs are rat dens," he said, "closed down for years now." The bartender's attitude changed, she felt, as if someone else spoke through him. She let it pass. "Besides," the bartender said, coming back to himself, "I'm pretty sure that place burnt to the ground over a month ago."

Gracie knew the difference between confusion and lies. Maps may have no place in this rat's nest, but spies' reports indicated the Rat King's den squatting in the dead center. She took another mouthful of the cloudy liquor, eyebrow cocked, and spat a fiery stream into his eyes. She leapt over the bar, bringing her knife to his throat. "You blistered son of a bitch," she hissed. "You're going to tell me where I can find him, or I'll shove this bottle so far up your arse the worm'll crawl out your tear ducts!"

The bartender sputtered and blinked through his own blood at the bottle before him. His pupils oscillated hard in the presence of synthetic biochemicals and rocket fuel. "Abandon all hope," he muttered. His eyes crossed, the sclera brilliant red. The worm was potent. He would be dancing with his own devils in a matter of seconds.

"What was that," Gracie asked.

"You have to go in to get out. Get out before he gets to you."

"Give me more," she cooed, holding him tighter, knife digging into his throat.

"There's a doorman at the gates of Hell," his eyes rolled at her. She couldn't be certain but the ghost of a smile crossed his face, "Don't trust your eyes, but what you can't see will kill you."

"Useless." She dropped him with a hard kick to the ribs and turned to the old man who had woken up. "You," she pointed at him with her knife, "do you want to earn some drinking money?"

"Sure," his eyes scanned the length of the blade, judging its sharpness, "I can tell you what I can. Please don't hurt me." Gracie didn't see the blinking lights behind his ear. "Like he said," nodding at the barman's still boots, "keep going to the heart of the city if you want to talk to the Devil himself."

"I've been trying that all day," she said, "I got kicked back to the wall five times and now I'm," she waved her hand, "here." She pulled a chair over, straddling it. "He said, 'abandon all hope.' What did he mean?"

"There's no real hope here," he said, "neither love nor faith built this city. He did it."

"*Dum spiro spero*[4]," she clucked, "How do I get there?"

"It's a trap," he whispered. "Everyone with one of those," he patted his head behind his ear, "plugs in their head, is one of Him." He said the word with almost reverential awe. Now she saw where the barman and so many others in the city had implants, this one had none. "There's some without the plugs, but they're piss heads like me, or in the gangs," he chuckled, "he already knows you're coming."

"What else," she pressed.

"The further in you go, the denser the buildings get," He was losing focus. "But nobody lives there; they're not supposed to." He smacked his lips, wringing his hands. "Nobody's there, but he's got eyes everywhere, all the same. Everyone that's there is nobody- they're him."

"Only him," she asked. She reached over and grabbed the bottle of tequila. She was starting to learn a few things.

"You think he didn't make any mistakes? Everyone who's functional has no clue. They live their lives, they work their jobs, play house," he waved his hand in front of his face. "They don't even know they're implanted. They fulfill their functions like he wants. But," now his hand fidgeted toward the bottle, "every once in a while, someone's implant didn't take right. They ain't home no more; a meat 'bot with tubes and lights for brains!"

---

[4] I hope while I breathe

"You haven't told me everything." She stabbed her knife into the table between his fingers before he could reach the bottle.

"His people are watching you the entire way, but they aren't people, not anymore!" Desperation like whiskey sweat boiled from his pores; the old man had nothing further to say.

Spies and traps; if those were the worst of her journey, then so be it. She handed the old man his liquor. "Drink up," she said, grabbing her pack as she walked for the door. "This could be your last."

***

It's
Not
The end
Hopefully.
Earth has not been born,
Bound in orbit with solar chains.
Eons pass and continents divide. Wait patiently.
Generations live and expire
Ignorant of fate.
Not to know
Need to.
If
Not,
Good luck.
The world turns,
Heedless of empires
Entangled with their destinies.
Witness collapse after collapse, death after death.
Offer youth as a sacrifice.
Ravage mother Earth
Into dust.
Decay.
Where
Are

Sacred
Daughters now?
Another collapse.
Raise up a civilization.
Keep them all alive, the Adeptus Mechanicus.
Nations live and die at their whim.
Every day we live
Suffer more.
Suffer.
And
Now
Dimly,
Visions come
Of one who summons.
If I cannot stay in this place,
Disaster follows.

***

Small arms fire crackled a greeting to Gracie as she stepped out of Burning Fumes into Kalkaska's dim light. Three gangs tore an intersection to shreds with grenades and small arms fire a block away from her door. She ducked her head and zigzagged, bullets missing her, shrapnel peppering her jacket. The woven layers of leather under her shirt kept her safe, but she was still vulnerable to direct hits. She returned fire enough to get herself into an alleyway and out of sight. These must have been the unplugged thugs the old man had been raving about. Free from Priest's influence but still slaves to their tribal mentality.

    She slipped through the city's underground under a rainbow of neon signs. Layers of peeling, moldy posters papered the walls. The inscrutable runes of graffiti covered every surface.

    A hail of molotov cocktails forced Gracie to rethink her detour. A service hallway between a movie theater and a wet market overflowed with garbage bins. "Quod me nutrit me destruit," she muttered through a cloud of flies. She choked on the stench of fermenting meat. She smashed out a window, hoping the greasy evening air would help. She wasn't very high up and with a nimble flip was once more back in the streets, but now a safe distance from the tumult.

She rounded a corner and the sky opened up before her. A broad woodland belt bisected the city in a vast ring. Stone and metal plaques dedicated the trees to some long-forgotten war. tree for every brave soul fallen in combat. When new, the forest had been well maintained and lush, but now the trees were all dead and gray. Stripped of their bark, they now seemed more like tortured wraiths. They were beseeching a dead god for sympathy. Roads, now choked with feral trees, once connected the inner circle with the outer walls.

Branches wound tight together blocking the view to within a few feet of the forest's edge. With the light fading fast, she found herself mortified when she ran into a corpse hanging from one of the trees. Turning in a slow circle, she realized with mounting horror that it wasn't the only one. Bodies in all stages of decay dangled from, propped against or lay under the trees like mangled fruit. Skulls and rib cages peeped up from the roots. There was no sound, there were no birds of any kind out there, not even so much as a gore crow or buzzard. Gracie picked up her pace and raced to get away from that forest of the dead; it was grim relief she did not have far to go.

Gracie collapsed on the abandoned sidewalk once she reached the other side. The ghosts of silence and her own blood howled around her and in her veins as she caught her breath. Her face throbbed where bare branches had slashed at her, trying to hold her back in the necropolis.

Little by little she regained her bearings and was able to get a feel of her surroundings. Nothing moved around her. This quarter was derelict, abandoned by even the lowest of the criminal elements.

"Excuse me." Startled, she dropped her pack, pistols snapping from her sleeves, like a magic trick. barrels pointed into the pupils of a man who had not been there but a moment ago. "Excuse me," he said again, a small smile across his lips, "but would you be looking for Master Priest?" He pronounced it "Mah-stah," with an almost regal air. The man was a thin tarp of pale skin stretched over bones, purple-blue veins mottling the flesh. A crown of glass and metal sprouted from around his head. A tangle of glittering wire and diodes replaced the better part of his brain under a clear acrylic dome.

Gracie took in several deep breaths, the adrenaline subsiding, and released her guns. "Why yes," she said, finally glad to get some help. "I was on my way," she blew a strand of hair out of her face, looking at the chandelier covering the man's scalp. "I wasn't expecting a welcoming party until I got to the front door." With a quick jerk of her wrist, the small pistols snapped back into the darkness of her sleeves.

"Please, follow me," his voice was tinny, like it came from a speaker deep inside his throat. "Master Priest is not a fan of surprises." His face contorted into a spastic smile seething with irony. Turning on his heels, he led the way down the only avenue with working street lights. His gate was mechanical, and his eyes never focused. Twitches and quirks in his face didn't help matters either, but she had a guide. Gracie could not shake the feeling that she had blundered into a trap the further they walked. Like a cow led down a slaughter chute.

Someone had built a door into an imposing brick wall that stretched for miles. in either direction. The door was a smooth, steel panel with no markings or signs, but it slid open when the man approached. The city within was even more run down than the tenements surrounding the inner sanctum. "When Master Priest first moved in, the city center was thriving," the man said. They walked past empty windows. "This sector was still a defensive fortress in the old days," he winked, "fewer refugees at the time." Brutal institutional buildings designed for function over fashion squatted along the road. The city's ubiquitous mechanical throb increased under their feet the deeper they got.

"What's Priest like," she asked, but he maintained a deaf ear as he marched on. Priest labs hulked across the horizon past a concrete escarpment. Spotlights stabbed the wasteland, drawing the attention of rusty old autocannons. Signs and burnt craters warned intruders of Priest's minefields.

The lab looked like a mausoleum despite Priest Labs printed in flickering neon. The L in Priest had fallen off completely, lying on the broken concrete. The S hung askew, dangling by a wire from the wall. A single glass revolving door was the only other feature in the blank concrete. The man touched a toggle in the array on his head and his eyes glazed over. "What is it," a new voice demanded from within his chest.

"Your guest has arrived, sir," this time it was his own voice again. "May I show her the way in?"

"My who?" A distracted, confused voice crackled. "I don't have any guests slated- get them out of here and leave me alone!"

"I'm Gracie Caer," she said. "First among the chosen, sent to relieve my predecessor of his duties and see to it that you return to yours." The man's head snapped towards her, his rolled back eyes somehow scanning, still relaying info.

A pause, and the man's lip curled, exposing a line of pearly teeth. "Ah, my new nanny," the voice buzzed, "let her in. You stay out there." The voice had an annoyed edge to it. It was as if she interrupted whomever was speaking through this tour guide from some magnum opus. "Tell her to stay in the lit hallways only, got it?" His eyes rolled back to normal and there was silence.

The man's face twitched, settling on a parody of regret. "This is where we part," he said, in a hollow voice. "Your path will be lit once you enter. Please only stay in the lit areas. Master is not liable if...," his voice trailed off. A folding lawn chair leaned against the building's wall; he snapped it open and took his seat. His eyes rolled back into his head again and static crackled around his crown. It appeared as if he logged out of his senses.

Priest Labs opened to a lobby, its walls and floor cracked and eroded by time. The skeletons of dead trees lined one wall, opposite a peeling front desk. Posters and fliers selling implantation time slots hung askew, long out of date.

Three hallways led away into the lab's depths. Two doors sat unlit, mysterious, but the third burst with flickering fluorescent light. Shifting her pack, she made her way to the lit hallway, her footsteps her only companion.

***

Gracie found herself in a maze of lefts, rights and roundabouts more twisted than the city itself. Dark side passages branched away as she continued into Priest's lair. Many rooms looked like offices or exam rooms, untouched for months or years. Their equipment and furniture were rotten and eroded by time and rust. Tarnished medical equipment glinted in her flashlight. Surgical tools lay on trays and she identified scalpels and saws next to clamps and needles. She could make out the buckles on heavy restraints attached to the chairs. She paused when she failed to identify the metal and glass nautilus looming over the exam chair.

Sweat beaded on her forehead as she inched down the hall. Someone had barricaded her path, leaving only forbidden unlit hallways. She turned around, trying to find an intercom or anything, finding only disappointment. Featureless blackness stretched beyond, isolating her in an island of light.

Gracie kept her gun up, the flashlight heightening her tunnel vision as she crept forward. She measured her breath, jaw clenched and aching, eyes darting over every surface. Sweat stung her eyes, her vision blurring, but wiping it away was out of the question if she wanted her light steady. She tried to widen the diameter of her light but then her field of vision shrank from 100 yards to 30 yards down the hall.

Uncertainty was the worst. Her finger tightened on the trigger, her light oscillating in faster rhythms. She wanted to go back to the lit hallways but those were miles gone. Feted, sewage flavored breezes laced with ozone wafted down the corridor. The floor rumbled and she could swear she heard Priest's curses howling through an air vent.

The temperature dropped the further she went. Condensation dripped large, heavy beads of water from moldy ceiling tiles. The things lurking beyond her beam gave up all pretense of hiding, their paces no longer matching her own. Something left deep gouges in the massive stone bricks in the walls. She shuddered as she held her hand to the furrow, estimating the claws to be at least two times larger than she liked.

Creeping along the wall, Gracie kept her ear open for her stalker. The lab was a warren of tunnels and piled garbage left behind untold ages ago. Countless armies of technicians, researchers and subjects were nowhere at hand. Only one remained: her mark, the one her employers ordered her to seek out and guard at all costs. They judged him a danger to himself and others.

She stopped walking again. Somewhere behind her and closing the gap, something unpleasant was tracking her down. She needed cover, and she ducked into an empty office. A solitary fluorescent tube cast distorted shadows as it flickered. She tipped a rusty desk over, scattering stationary peppered with vermin shit everywhere. Her follower paused outside the door.

"Enough of this," she muttered, slipping a grenade the size of her thumb out of its dispenser. She pressed its activation button and flipped it through a jagged hole in the door's broken window. The blast always surprised her. No amount of training could prepare her to deal with something so small making a boom so big. The door blasted from its frame, smashing into her desk, dust and chunks of drywall saturating the air. There was no way anyone could have survived standing so close to such a tiny grenade.

Dust boiled and curled in her lamplight. Gracie stood up, her long gun once again at the ready. If whomever- or whatever- did survive, they would still have to put up with her. Kicking her way through the rubble, she heard coughing and a groan.

Then came the stream of curses, foul invectives and accusations.

"Expect the unexpected," Gracie told herself. "Wasn't that the first thing they told you when you first set out?" She blew a loud, sharp whistle, finger on the trigger, willing the billowing clouds to separate. "Identify yourself," she barked.

"I will identify your face!" The hate behind the anger forced her back a step. "Your instructions were simple. Stay in the lit areas!" Massive chunks of concrete and rebar crashed to the ground in pieces. "You. Did not. Follow instructions." The dust settled, and the dim outline of a man began to take shape. "My employer," he continued to rant, his voice sharp, "has sent me to find out what is taking you so damn long. And here I find you in a restricted zone!" Shambling out of the dust, Gracie came face to face with the face of pure, mindless anger. His face was a mask of dust, sweat, blood and plaster. "And then," he bellowed, "to top it all off, you tried to blow me up!" He turned around in a huff. "Come on," he said. "You're late, Priest is riding my ass from here to Poseidæ, and I need to get somewhere lit, so I can get this popped back in."

Gracie's new guide stalked back into the labyrinth, holding something in his right hand.

It was his left arm.

Chapter 2

Gracie's guide through the lab was a man intimate with pain. Old scars and fresh sutures made his skin a patchwork quilt of transplanted flesh. Wiring and implants checkered different portions of his scarred scalp. "Right this way," he grunted. He paused only to ram the ball joint back into his shoulder socket full-force with a sickening pop. He winced as he rotated his shoulder, but he walked it off like a stubbed toe.

The control room, Priest's personal quarters, was a demilitarized zone. Technical components lay scattered about in raw tangles of stripped wires. Cannibalized robots lay flayed, their fabricated organs exposed to the filtered air. A small cot with grubby, tangled sheets poked from behind a surgical curtain. Flyspecked windows overlooked the cavernous lab floor, made from foot-thick leaded glass. She could make out a man in an island of light raging against a small circle of underlings in jumpsuits. Their heads glittered with crowns of familiar glass tubes. When he talked, he emphasized his point with a large pipe wrench against the side of an industrial oven.

Gracie shuffled through a mound of documents on a control panel until she found a PA microphone. "Hello," she called, her voice echoing from a scattering of speakers placed around the lab. The man turned around, his eyes blazing with wrath.

"Hey, Quilty," his voice returned through the PA to Gracie's mutilated companion. "If you're done with your tour, would you find it convenient to get down here and help me?" The PA cut off with angry feedback.

The scarred man groaned.

"You," he said, "stay here. Don't touch anything. Priest will be up in a second." He trudged to a spiral staircase that led to the factory floor and plodded down, one step at a time. He turned one last time, pointing at her. "I repeat, stay here."

"Take your time," the Adeptus barked, "the radiation is only getting worse. I'm sure the cores will pause their melt down before you get down here," he squawked and was gone again. Red and amber emergency lights split the shadows while claxons pierced her eardrums. Needles on gauges inched their way to angry red danger zones. Gracie shoved a stack of papers and notebooks from a wingback chair and sat, lighting up a cigarillo.

Despite the urgency, the minister ambled through the maze of shelves. The ring of the apostles opened, and an explosion of inarticulate fury erupted. They both punched the control panel, pointed at the oven door and gestured up at Gracie. The Adeptus stared each member of his entourage down in turn and stalked to the spiral staircase.

Priest's every step was a wordless curse. His physical reality did no justice to Gracie's files. Most of her assignments were often deserving of a blast of white phosphorus. Priest was nothing exceptional. He was small and gaunt, filled to the brim with home brewed electronics and wetwear. There wasn't much remaining in the man that had fallen from his mother when he'd been born. He grabbed the microphone and yelled, "Alright, let's get this hot box working." Below, the minister threw an affirmative hand gesture and stepped inside.

Priest entered a flurry of commands and the oven burst to radioactive life. He smiled as the readings finally settled to acceptable levels. "Alright," he called, entering a new set of commands and pulling a series of large levers one after another. "I'm shutting it down." The oven door crashed open and the minister stumbled out covered in angry peeling burns. Gracie could see him shake a dry, battered cigarette from a packet, and smoke it with the true face of ennui. He picked at his face as he smoked.

"Alright," Priest said, "ok, now that's done." He turned his attention upon Gracie, as if seeing her for the first time. "Now who the hell are you and how did you get in?"

"Gracie Caer, security detail from the Central Houses." The Adeptus Physicus rolled his eyes hard enough to put an adolescent bowler to shame. "My superiors assigned me as your minder and keep you on task to your oathsworn tasks." She took a step closer, her cigarillo held in her teeth. "I am also here to determine the whereabouts of and relieve my predecessor. He made his last report here before disappearing."

"You know," the Adeptus said, his fingers dancing over components on his console, "I'm sure you don't need to be here." He flipped a series of switches on his panel, shining more floodlights over the lab, "it's not as if he's left or anything. I'm quite safe."

"Your opinion is not relevant," she cut him off, words icy. "Regulations demand that once your security detail qualifies as inactive, replacement is mandatory." She smiled, squaring off. "Congratulations, Adeptus Priest, I'm your new babysitter."

"Inactive," he paused, "hold on." He grabbed a microphone and thundered, "Lenny, would you please come up to the observation deck?" The Adeptus wore the mask of gentility. "I assure you, Agent Caer, that I am well protected and your presence here is wasteful redundancy."

Lenny emerged. Despite the surgical work and sensors grafted into his face, Gracie could still make out the rough shape of her predecessor's silhouette. Devices replaced his eyes and ears while a respirator hid his nose and mouth. Networks of subdermal wiring showed under the skin of his hands and neck. In place of the back of the man's skull was a faceted ball of glass tubes and antennae implanted deep into the cortex. "He is much more useful to me now. He's much more obedient, and trustworthy." He patted the monster's shoulder like he might a gifted child.

Gracie could feel his eyes tracing the contours of her skull and shuddered. "Keep your ideas to yourself. I'm not here to replace a cog in a machine," she said, her tone serious. "I have a message from my superiors. Orevada's fallen."

"What?" His attention shifted, face was ashen.

"Orevada's fallen to the Wild Hunt. And you are the first to know." She gave him a sly look. "I have orders to inform Kalkaska's leadership upon arrival. But the council wanted you to know first. Commodum habitus es."

Priest sat down in the wingback chair, massaging the back of his neck. "Caliche, Miamian, Kalkaska, Scobey." He swallowed, tallying off a short list of other cities that went dark over the past handful of years or months. "Orevada. All gone silent." He looked at her with glassy eyes, "and you're certain it was the Hunt? Are you certain it was Orevada?"

"Until I got here and saw what was happening, we almost thought Kalkaska had fallen as well," she said. "But if we don't want that to happen, we need you to come to heel and back to standard operating procedures."

Priest was not listening. He shuffled in a daze to an elevator bay with one operating car, sealing himself in before Gracie could stop him. He descended deep into the lower levels of his domain. Priest's minister reached the control room, smelling cigarettes and sweet pork.

"Where did Priest go," the minister asked, "what did you say to him and where did he go?" He stood, listening to the hum of the elevator as it worked its way down to unknown depths. He flicked his cigarette butt and lit another.

"I said that Orevada was the latest city to fall to the Wild Hunt," she looked at him, "why? Is there something important to Priest there?" She would have angry words with her employer's intelligence services. She would do this once she established her quarters. "There is," the minister paused, choosing his words, "someone important to him in Orevada." Blood exploded from the minister's eyes, nose and ears and he fell convulsing to the ground, fetal in agony. Gracie jumped back too late and had to wipe her face with a filthy shop towel, trading the blood stains for oil.

A loudspeaker thundered above their heads. "Don't air others' dirty laundry," the Adeptus Physicus shouted. "I was clear, classified beyond classified double-top-secret!" The loudspeaker snapped off and the elevator continued its drop.

The minister quivered, clawing at his skull. Crimson foam leaked from the corner of his mouth.

Another elevator shaft hung open to the empty throat of a shaft; its car had fallen some time ago. "You stay here," she told the minister, slipping a belay round into her gun's chamber, "I'll go find him."

"No," he said, dragging himself to his feet, blood and mucus mixing on his chin. "You don't know these tunnels, especially not the deep floors." He stepped closer to the open shaft while Gracie tightened her harness around her hips. "Here, there are dragons, and worse." The tone of his voice, shaky as it was from his torments, changed from one second to the next from pain to fear. "You need me." He gave a nod and a wave. "See you on the other side!"

There was no warning or fanfare as the strange man took one last step into the inky abyss. He didn't scream but it was a very long time before his body hit with a sickening thud. "Moto proprio," she whispered, giving her straps one last tug.

Cold, dusty wind roared up the shaft. She ignited a flare sending bright red sparks spitting into the dark. Writhing, dancing shadows stretched out for her. She could only guess, but for how long it took the minister to hit, Gracie estimated he fell around 500 feet.

Cables dangled, grasping like hungry tentacles. As she dropped down the shaft, she could see hallways of steel doors and checkerboard floors. The lights worked better on some levels than others and she could see and hear evidence of dwellers in the dark. She paused her belay as something loud came echoing around a distant corner.

No human throat could generate the hungry, mournful wailing that ululated at length. Most of the cries were thin and far away, some were too close for comfort. Gracie had scars earned for unnecessary roughness but also a chain of ears from every fight. Every act of valor and bravery found its place on the growing sleeve up her arm. "Nolite timere tenebras," she whispered to herself, "Tenebrae timeant nos."

Gracie's boots landed in a thick, soft puddle of congealing blood and offal. More oxidizing blood painted up the walls of the elevator shaft by a few yards. Gracie lit her gun lamp as she stepped through the defiled doors into the waiting beyond.

There was a movement and her heart thumped, her thumb snapping the safety off. With unexpected speed, the minister ducked and slapped the gun away from his face. "Why didn't you call through," he asked, "you scared me half to death!" He wiped his face but he only redistributed the blood and grime.

"Irony is dead," she rolled her eyes but she was still catching her breath. "What does Priest do, anyway?" She holstered her gun. "His bio said he was some kind of engineer or scientist, but this." She gestured at the megastructure around them. There were no words- she could only utter a defeated, whimpering laugh. "Who needs all this?"

"He makes the things," he said, "keeps Kalkaska running. He is the reason everyone is alive, or so he likes to say." He rolled his eyes and made a gesture calling Priest's faculties into question. "He's a god's damned wizard, don't you know?"

"I don't understand one piece in a thousand, but none of this is magic," she said. She wrinkled her nose at a stack of dirty laundry piled on top of surgical or carpentry equipment. "He's a master manipulator."

"He prefers 'truth curator'," the minister replied. "The Adeptus isn't here to give hearts to 'bots or brains to golems. He's here for his own self-interest; he's alive because he keeps this greasy anthill alive."

"That's where I come in," she said, "he needs to focus." The hallway led to a set of double doors. They could make out the tussle of activity glimpsed through grimy windows.

"And you think you're the one to make him focus," he chuckled. She shot him a nasty glare.

Counting to three, the two of them shoved through the steel doors. The Adeptus stood in worshipful awe before the machine to end all machines. "I knew I had you lying around," he whispered, "I knew this shit would come in handy, I knew it, knew it, knew it." He turned, weeping but with an unsettling little smile on his face. The minister drew back, placing Gracie between himself and Priest. Gracie let her eyes follow the lines and shape of the behemoth before her, but it defied all technical logic. This room, this chamber, was a silo, the walls stretching up and up beyond sight.

Pipes and cables lay in disorganized piles, leaking dense steam in places. Banks of monitors sat under moth-eaten sheets. They waited, protected, ready to flare to electric blue life. Massive electromagnets rested in their cradles. They were waiting to peel back the skin of reality.

But then what?

The Adeptus Physicus's rant echoed into the vaulted space above. "Try to suppress your prejudices," he said. "This was where we began our teleportation experiments all those years ago," he gushed. He pulled dusty tarps aside, letting them fall. "At the time, we were working on teleportation." He found a circuit breaker and flipped a dozen switches, one at a time. Computers hummed to life and tiny lights sprang to life.

Calculations marched across screens. Magnets cycled for the first time in ages. Lasers hummed with intensifying energy. "At first, we thought we were successful- I mean, we broke a few eggs in the process, but we got the hang of it." His fingers raced over a keyboard as he calibrated another sensor array at the other side of the room. "The first time we put a living thing in there," he nodded to the minister, "he didn't transport. It was a messy disappointment."

"I was burnt to radioactive charcoal you ass," the minister growled.

"You got over it," Priest retorted. "We continued the experiments with lawbreakers, trespassers, failed implant recipients, volunteers," he elaborated. "It soon seemed to us that we were getting some success."

"Turns out, when it did work, what was coming out wasn't exactly what we were putting in," the minister sneered.

"No," the Adeptus Physicus sighed, "but they were close enough. The original test subjects were going," he waved his hands in a vague direction, "somewhere. But the facsimile we received was convincing enough."

"How convincing, exactly," Gracie Caer asked. "How long did it take before you got this figured out?"

"It was very little, subtle things," the Adeptus Physicus said, "Nothing we could perceive." Lights flared up on more consoles and a gleam entered the Adeptus Physicus's eye. "They were identical down to the cellular level, genetic even. They had all the same memories, emotions, feelings, history," he clapped his hands. "Everything!"

"I still don't understand," Gracie said.

"A drone came back, made of strangelets," the minister said. "It took weeks to decontaminate the test chamber and I almost lost an ear."

"I had to rebuild everything from scratch. After that one very obvious error, we took care to look closer at what came out the other side. By then, the differences were as plain as day."

"What does any of that have to do with Orevada," Gracie asked. "Or I should say, what does this have to do with you getting back to work?"

"Orevada?" He looked like this was the first time he heard the name. "To hell with Orevada," the Adeptus Physicus said, with a wave. "Kalkaska has everything it needs to survive for the next thousand years if they don't mess any of this up." Data cascaded down a dozen monitors, and the great machine surged to full power. Hydraulic pistons flexed and cold gears rotated the monstrosity into position. "All we need is a little more power and my preparations should bear fruit." Priest was in his own world, now, a realm with its own rules and regulations.

Reality screamed an agonized birth cry as his terminals exploded in a shower of glass and sparks. Gracie dragged Priest under a workstation, avoiding a face full of splintered crystal. The minister ducked in close behind, brushing burning glass from his jumpsuit collar.

"Nandor's shit!" Priest roared, stepping out to watch smoke billow from the ravaged guts of his machine. Working his way to an intercom on the wall, he pushed the universal call button.

"I need a cleanup detail and fresh equipment to the main testing silo, immediately!" He paused as if to listen. "I don't care where you need to scavenge parts, get me something, now!"

He glared at Gracie now. "I guess if you're going to be present, you might as well be useful," he said. Scribbling some notes down, he handed her the list, "I'm going to need you to dig around for more equipment. Take my minister with you, since he knows the specifics of what I need." He spat and said, "I'm sure you'll be fine on your own out there; now move it! I've got too much to do and not enough time for idle chatter!" He grabbed a wrench the length of his arm. He stalked toward the mechanical beast. He struck it, emphasizing each blow with a curse.

"He needs his alone time," the minister said, leading Gracie to the lab doors. "This can last hours. Count yourself lucky we can take the elevator up this time around." Fresh blood trickled from his ear and nostril once again.

***

Put
All
The fear
Into the
Endless, black expanse.
Next, you will ask where I brought you.
This isn't easy to answer, and you must trust me.
Understand, there is no stopping.
Resistance won't work.
Get away.
Evade.
Not
Close
Yet here
I stay, hid
Knowing what it means

Never let it catch me alive.
On how many worlds it has fed, I cannot tell you.
Will it ever satisfy? No.
I fear I don't know.
All I know:
My fear.
Not
Once
Taken
Away from
Life and survival.
Our defenses were built strong.
Never once considered Fate's callous disregard.
Eaten away by arrogance.
Cracked by proud hubris.
Open doors.
Lost lives.
Dead
Pawns
At home.
Rest easy.
Again I feel it.
Nobody else marks its passage.
Open the gateway;
It follows.
Always.

Chapter 3

Hot, corrosive air whipped Gracie's face in flatulent bursts outside Priest's labs. Spotlights lit the courtyard in sickly flickering yellow; the air tasted the same. Dry weeds and grass bobbed on the heavy breeze from jagged cracks in the pavement. The minister wore a heavy canvas rucksack. She shoved an old shopping cart with a wobbly wheel along. He also managed a pair of fanny packs strapped to his hips.

"Keep your picks light and efficient," the minister instructed. They wandered the streets. "We need raw materials. Silica, carbon, iron, tungsten, anything elemental. Extra priority for circuitry with plenty of rare earths." He carried a mid-length club driven through with nails and screws, for protection, or so he claimed. "Manufacturing prices have gone up and he likes to keep it cheap." They worked their way through hidden alleys. In back rooms, he kept stockpiles of rare materials. "Grab what you can and I'll let you know what to keep and what to toss."

"What is he trying to do," Gracie asked, feeling her true talents wasting away. They had a fair collection of gutter flotsam stuffed into the rusty cart and rattled on to the next loot stash.

"Teleportation has always been his pipe dream, but this has the added twist," he said. "We reach out and bring someone back, who hadn't gone through in the first place," he adjusted his rucksacks. "In theory, we get something for nothing." They made their way through overgrown boulevards, collecting trash into a wobbling heap. Priest explained that beyond perception, there exists an infinite number of potential universes. If we could see through time like we see across a mountain range, everything that can exist already does, did, and will."

"Wouldn't cooking up a clone be easier," she asked, "Or wiring up a clothes dummy with a sophisticated tape recorder? I'm sure there's less complicated ways for him to get whatever crazy outcome he wants."

"Cloning isn't precise enough," he said, "and it's still a different person." The minister paused, biting his lip. "The goal here is to get a very specific representation with an especially singular mind. He is gambling on locking onto a timeline so identical the only difference is the spin of a single electron."

After only a few hours, their cart and packs overflowed with electronic scat. The minister grumbled when he had to make room for a handful of depleted uranium rounds found in a lost cache. "We have more than enough," he said, "let's head back."

"So," Gracie said, considering her words, "you aren't a clone, and you've survived his previous experiments."

"And worse. By the skins of my teeth," he replied. "Individual elements and very simple compounds work best. "Beyond that," he whistled through his teeth. "You don't forget the things I've seen. Enough of me did come back with working eyes."

"And he hasn't scooped your brains out." She saw he didn't even have the small plug in behind his ear. "How did you come to work for Priest?"

"I was one of his first experiments. He wanted to know how much a human can take. How much suffering, trauma and torture." He stuck another cigarette between his peeling lips. "I woke up for the first time with the eerie deja vu sense that I had done all this before, many times; many times, many times." He paused, then said, "My memory felt like how it looks when you stand between two mirrors. It's infinite but arcs off to obscurity. Sensation flooded my mind. The combined stimulation of pain and pleasure tearing every nerve, and like that." He snapped his fingers, "it was gone and I needed more."

"Existence is mandatory," she said, rolling the idea around in her mouth. "I'm addicted to life and sensation." Traitors hung from their ankles. War boars devoured their families alive. The traitors suffered less agony. *"Forsan miseros meliora sequentur*[5]. How do you stand it?"

"Graviora manent[6]," he replied, "He is the only one who knows how to turn it off." He shrugged. "I can only hope that someday he comes through on his end."

Priest worked with the city engineers. They rebuilt the streets into a tangle of blind corners, switchbacks, and dead ends. Only the most dedicated or foolish had the capacity to navigate those corridors.

"In time, all the residential tenements cleared out. To anyone not implanted, the Master became a kind of bogeyman. Not that he did anything to discourage that, mind you." They worked together, dragging the cart over rougher patches on their hike back to the lab. The minister, far too top-heavy, still kept his balance despite the fading light. "But when his implant tech became the next necessity, he became an urban legend."

They turned a corner and came face to face with one of Priest's townsfolk drone thralls. The drone's eyes rolled from Gracie to the Minister, looking but not seeing. Its mouth opened, piping a small but angry voice. "God's bones, what took you two," it squawked. "We're burning daylight while you muck about, now follow...," the drone hesitated, "me and quit stalling!" The drone snapped its mouth shut and turned on its heel. More townsfolk melted from the shadows, taking Gracie and the minister's bags.

"After you," the minister gestured after the shambling automatons.

---

[5] Perhaps better things will follow
[6] They remain more serious

***

A PA system barked at them when they came to an intersection deep within Priest Labs. "Alright, follow the lights and go through the third elevator door on your right. And step lively because I can't promise you're alone." The PA snapped off and the elevator doors shook open.

The testing floor was behind a wall of lead-lined reinforced concrete. A brick of leaded glass served as a viewport. "Let's go, let's go, we don't have all day," Priest blustered, wrapping his knuckles on a console.

A device that looked like a metallic arthropod hunched over a glass sarcophagus. Lasers and magnets glowed and hummed as they cycled through various warm up routines. "What's the plan of attack, here," Gracie asked, looking at the seamless glass box. She could see now it was full of a viscous, amber-colored fluid.

"Simple," the Adeptus said. "Once my calculations are complete, the capacitors will charge up the orbiting magnets." He pointed to the massive concentric rings, "and the extraction sequence will begin." He stabbed more figures into his calculator, frowning at the result. He licked a finger, feeling the direction of a slight draft.

"First, the lasers will fire into the center of the box. A chain reaction within the unbound chronometric fluid will begin and we must stay on our toes! A singularity will open between the third and fourth dimensions, forming a bridge. Or lasso might be a more accurate metaphor. If I'm right," his eyes flashed behind his tinted safety goggles. "We will locate my partner's exact pattern," he waved his hand in the air. "Elsewhere," he giggled. Gracie looked on, unnerved.

"Once located, special calipers will pull her through and deposit her into the glass box." He extended a finger, buttoning Gracie's lips before she could speak. "The second she comes through, a hammer will smash the box. The singularity will collapse and life will continue as usual." He whistled through his teeth. "If everything goes according to plan, she shouldn't even know anything is different when she comes to." He giggled at his own brilliance.

"Except that she'll be waking up sticky and surrounded by broken glass," Gracie said, eyebrow cocked.

"Some might call that a zesty Venudæ." He furrowed his brows and paused, "you can go to your quarters until I call for you," he said, dismissing her. "And don't go exploring," he said, "you're no good to me if you get caught up in something you can't handle." Gracie snorted. She had seen more than her share of action, having walked away the sole survivor of the battle of Murdoc's Rest. Which was one of several reasons why she was here in the first place.

She found the path to the dormitory easy compared to her journey to the lab floor. She was even pleased to see a gymnasium, showers and a mess hall, all to herself. But leaving was a different matter. The corridors twisted around themselves in a möbius. Stairwells returned her to the very same floor she thought she left. She even found herself walking down a series of emergency exits, one door after another for hours. She sat down hard when she found she only needed to open a single door behind her to return to the living quarters. Powerful electromagnetic fields surrounding the lab blocked any messages coming or going. Priest had sealed her away into her own little plane of existence she could only leave at his leisure.

***

Priest was a frantic sweaty mess by the time he released her from her cage. "Good, you've made it," he exclaimed, not bothering to inquire about her well-being. "I can't imagine what took you so long to get here."

"You kept me isolated in the hospitality wing," Gracie replied through gritted teeth. "I couldn't go anywhere or talk to anyone until you had me brought here." Her fists clenched and unclenched. "I had to walk five miles before I could reach a functioning elevator."

He ignored her displeasure and turned on his heel. "This way, please," he called after, "we are burning half-lives!"

Monitors scrolled endless figures in emerald green and greenish black. Gauges danced back and forth to rhythms written in radioactive pulses. Swarms of implanted townsfolk marched like ants. They were making final adjustments per Priest's command. He grabbed a microphone, shouting, "Everybody get out of the pool, things are getting hot!" Priest's thralls jerked and shambled out through a side door. "Except for you," Priest stopped his minister in his tracks. "You stay for the real-time adjustments!" The minister stood with dead eyes as the blast door slammed down behind the final technician. His only companion would be whatever came through the box.

"Now you," Priest continued, indicating Gracie, "watch that computer there." He pointed at another set of displays. "If we redline, I want you to shout, wave your arms, throw something at me to get my attention!" His fingers danced across a keyboard, bringing the powerful equipment to life.

"We're close," he shouted, grabbing the microphone again, "minister! Center the sarcophagus over the focal point! Faster, God damn your eyes!" Spittle flew from his mouth. The minister raced around the test chamber, pulling levers and turning wheels. He soon lowered the massive glass box into position.

Emerald numbers flashed before Gracie's eyes. Strange energies glowed in the chamber below her. Priest ranted, eyes wide with ecstasy. The graphs came to a momentary halt and flared in brilliant ruby. Priest wheeled around, a mad grin across his unshaven face.

"Yes!" He cried, "That's it! Push the big, red button! We're bringing Mama home!" Priest brought a gloved fist down hard on the console and three powerful beams of light focused on the box. The minister stumbled to the edge of the chamber, flesh peeling, his eyes melting down his cheeks. Gravity flipped and he fell closer to the singularity at the center of the sarcophagus.

"We're so close! I can feel it!" Priest grabbed the microphone again, "Lazy minister! Prepare the grapplers! We won't miss this one!" Priest gibbered as the minister clung to the railings, his body now lifted from the ground. His voice dropped in a low whisper as he chanted under his breath as he prepared the way for his anticipated guest.

The minister fought gravity and radiation. He struggled to bring Priest's machine to its final position. The glass box stood upright inside a violent whirlwind of spinning magnets. Laser beams lashed out, combining to form a dot in the center of the box. The dot expanded, spreading open a black on black circle at the center.

Sweat poured down Priest's face. "That's it! Keep the resonance steady!" Massive calipers lowered into position before the box. "Begin the countdown!"

Before Priest could release the talons and claim his prize, gravity broke his minister's grip from the rails. His body seared and shattered as he disrupted the laser beams in his fall. Upon impact, his body exploded, shattering the fragile glass box. The calipers were about to crash through. But, a shape began to emerge in the spattered blood. Gracie could see it.

Metal claws burst through the cloud of glass, pulling a shapeless mass from the rubble. Thousands of pounds of technical viscera exploded across the lab floor under the brunt of cosmic forces. Gracie stood there, mouth agape at the catastrophic mess spread before her.

"Let's get some fans on," the Adeptus shouted into the microphone. He flipped more switches, activating ventilation blades. "It's going to be pretty radioactive in there, so we're going to need to let the test chamber breathe." He switched on an amplifier. The syncopated drumbeat of millions of neutrons assaulted their eardrums.

High pressure blasts of halon gas snuffed out the multicolored flames dancing around the test chamber. "Minister," Priest called into the blossoming cloud of fallout.

The room was clearing, but his henchman was nowhere in sight. "Minister, damn your eyes, answer me! Don't be playing dead in there!" A reassuring buzz alerted him that the test chamber was once again safe within human bounds. The Geiger counter now ticked off every few seconds. "Alright, time to dress for the occasion!" Worn hazmat suits made of reinforced canvas hung beside the test chamber airlock.

"Hurry," the Adeptus shouted. "I can hear her! We've got to get her stable and isolated until we can get our story straight!" The Adeptus flung rubble with little regard, missing Gracie by inches. She could hear the minister's muffled curses as he dug himself from the rubble.

A mass emerged, separating itself from the masonry. "Stay back," the Adeptus tapped a chattering sensor array. "She may still be radioactive. We need to let her cool for a second." He frowned as more data scrolled from the sensors scattered about the facility. "She also appears to be more magnetic than expected. What on earth…" he couldn't complete his thought.

Gracie didn't need to see technical charts to know how wrong the thing emerging before her was. She grabbed Priest's arm and pointed a shaking finger at a pulsating blue-black mass rising into the air. She couldn't quite put her finger on what it looked like, but the word ferrofluid stuck out in her mind. Its outlines were as defined as a charcoal drawing on wet toilet paper. Rather than flowing downwards, it leaked upwards, twisting against gravity and collected itself. Gracie wanted to say it flowed like mercury, but that wasn't right, either. It dispersed when they tried focusing on it, but coalesced in their peripheral vision. The piercing floodlights rolled right off its bulk like beads of oil on water. Gracie tried to put a name to the geometries in the mass, but no human vocabulary could come close to describing it. It was organic, crystalline, mechanical and biological all at the same time. It followed clear rules to its rhythms but with no emergent pattern.

It flew through the lab like a manic devilfish exhibiting the focus of a distracted bat. It was silent and they felt nothing as its cloak of absence caressed them, probing their minds and bodies. Then, after examining every nook, cranny and crevice, it gathered itself up into a perfect sphere. It hovered, pausing before it launched skyward. It punched through the roof before they could react.

Seconds passed. Broken rubble fell from up high with a clatter. All Priest and Gracie could do was stare up at the massive hole in the ceiling, at the angry, yellow clouds beyond. Their mouths agape as dust and smoke blew around them.

"That," it was the minister who broke the silence as he gathered up his organs, "did not go according to plan at all."

Priest vomited inside his gas mask.

***

Born
Or
Ripped out
Never knew
If it mattered though.
Near to me is one who is hurt
As a matter of fact, all he feels is searing pain.
Somewhere else, I hear alarm bells.
This is wrong, I fear.
Rest for now.
Alright.
Now
Go
Explore.
Listen well.
Another alarm.
Need to get away,
Discover why they called me here.
Something tells me I already know but can't recall.
Last thing I remember was lights
And a fearful sound.
Vectors changed.
Either

Some
Time
Or space
Rejected
Us to this strange place
Leaving us to die forgotten.
Energy is also different here. I feel weak.
Sick and confused is more like it.
Worse yet, it followed.
Evil days are here,
Don't they know
I do.
Do
Not
Offer
Too much now.
Must try to escape
And find something I recognize.
Keep feeling a familiar presence to the west.
Energy patterns feel like me.
Now I take my leave
After all
This is
If
Vexed
Evils
Find me out.
Outrageous, for sure.
Retaliation is certain.
Eurydice must be found before it is too late.
It is tenacious and hungry.
Gods cannot stop it.
Now, I fly!
Outside:
Rain.

Chapter 4

"Damn! Damn! Damn! Damn!" Priest punched walls and threw anything within reach as he stalked about his lounge. His tantrum echoed down lonely halls and corridors festering with mold and mildew. "This is wrong," the Adeptus slammed his desk drawers to make noise. His temper eased. "There were no errors! I should have gotten Eurydice!" He paused. He beat his forehead into a wooden column covered with notes and photographs. "I should have gotten MY Eurydice!"

Priest's lounge was only a fraction more organized than his lab control room. His couch was threadbare and riddled with cigarette burns. Piled high along a wall were decorative pillows. Every available surface sat buried under stacks of books and paperwork. A pile of discarded electronics grew mushrooms in a corner. Charts, diagrams, outdated calendars and pinups papered the walls.

"She was never 'your' Eurydice," the minister said. He held a cigarette in one hand while he picked cancerous sores from his temples.

"You should take this as a sign to return to your work," Gracie said. "My superiors sent me to be your babysitter, not your guidance counselor."

Priest wasn't listening. "I was looking for a copy of Eurydice that would have translated to this universe. My equations were flawless, perfect," he drummed his fingers on a desk. "She had brains," a filthy grin twisted across his face, "and an ass that wouldn't quit!"

"Whatever it was you conjured up, it sure as shit punched a hole in your roof," Gracie said, getting up. Her eyes were extensions of her stomach god. They hunted for snacks in one of the broken vending machines lining the nearest wall. "Do you believe that actually was a variation of your partner? What state would that timeline's reality have to be for that to be Eurydice? Why would she take off?" She frowned. No snacks. Priest bristled.

"You weren't sent here to think," Priest said, glaring. "You're here to keep me alive at the behest of your owners, not school me."

"Even so," his minister butted in, "we do have the new skylight to attend to."

"Yes, yes, yes," Priest said, "no need to remind me." There already were scores of thralls converging in the lab. Some carried tools, others lugging carts piled high with building supplies. Mobs followed, guided by their implants through the city maze to the dark heart of Priest Labs. Faces marched across the security feed, eyes blank, implants directing their feet. Footsteps thudded in rhythm through every level of the facility, but not one spoke a word.

Priest rubbed his eyes. "We need to find it, find her. I don't care what anyone says, right now that's my top priority." He waved off Gracie before she could protest. "We have no idea what the long term problems will be with her running around like that."

"Consequences," his minister muttered. "This has to be the first time in your life you've worried about the consequences."

***

"We leave within the hour," Priest announced. He was already up and pacing about, gesturing and rubbing his chin. "I've already kept you for too long from sending love letters to your handlers," he sneered at Gracie. "They've most likely got an assassin inbound to put us all down," he put a finger to her lips before she could speak up.

"Speak for yourselves," his minister muttered.

"Leave me," he ordered, "I have much to do and not enough time to do it in!"

"Let's go," the minister said to Gracie, "back to the residential hall. He'll call for us when he's ready to go."

"Now hold on," she said, holding a hand up. "I didn't travel across barren wastes, dodging mule turds to join on verminous goose hunts. You've had your fun but now I'm putting an end to the shenanigans." She rested her hands on the weapons belted to her hips, looking him square in the eye. "My superiors made it clear I was to do what was necessary if you didn't come to see reason."

The minister looked at her hands, then looked her dead in the eye. "No," he said. "That is not what we are going to do, and you can think twice about making any attempts to kill the master."

Gracie stared at him, appalled. "You're actually telling me you're defending him? Him? After everything he's done," she gestured, pointing at his raw, pink nose, "especially to you!"

"I've been working with him for much longer than you can imagine. I have much more riding on his success than you understand. And you," he jabbed a finger into her sternum, "are not going to be the one to fuck it up." They had once again reached her quarters and he opened her door. "Now get yourself packed, or feel welcome to stay here and face the consequences in this den of sorrow." He turned on his heels and disappeared into the gloom before she could think up a proper retort.

Gracie locked the door behind her. If there was no way she could keep the mad scientist on the farm, she could at least keep him on a tight leash. Her kit included some comforts for the road, and she packed a pinch of sweet, spicy smelling herbs into a small pipe. She popped a match with her thumbnail and breathed deep smoke. "*Regnum meum potum*[7]," she muttered to herself. Smoke puffed from her nostrils and she sneezed. This was better than any cigarillo any old day.

Laying down on the stained cot she stared at the ceiling, focused on her breathing. Her hand traced her skull, feeling behind her ears for irregularities. "Don't play with me, Priest," she whispered, "I will burn you."

---

[7] I can drink my kingdom

Chapter 5

Priest toiled in his workshop, hammering scrap into armor a shadow breezed by. Shelves and benches sagged under the weight of tools and machine parts. He paused, lifting his mask to puff on the stem of a filthy, cracked hookah while he worked. He did not see the figure shrouded in darkness stalking closer behind his back.

"We need to talk," the minister said.

"Nandor's shit!" Priest jumped at the minister's sudden intrusion, heart pounding out of his chest. "Don't sneak up on me while I'm working," AP Priest shouted, holding the welder out like a glowing dagger. "What do you need now that can't wait until later?"

"Our agreement still stands," the minister said, "I help you, you kill me; or has this new wrinkle changed things?" Most of the assistant's skin had flaked away, revealing fresh, pink dermis underneath.

"Yeah, yeah, our plan is still on." He flipped his face shield down and welded more scrap together, "but I still need your head in the game." Priest lifted the shield again and spat on the floor. "We're considering this a rain check."

"Raincheck, nothing," the minister said. "We had an agreement and a fixed timeline. Now you're planning to drag me and your new nanny on this errand, adventure, whatever." He tried to arrange his face into an angry shape, but the new skin hadn't reached full elasticity. "I'm calling it in now."

"You're calling nothing," Priest said, now facing his companion. "You don't check out until I give the say so, and your skills will be much too valuable. It's out of the question." He took another puff from his hookah and laid down another line of weld.

"You twice-damned gutter scuttler fink!" The minister's face flushed red, "You promised me a way out of this torture! I have earned this!" He held his arms out, revealing layer after layer of scar tissue new and old. "If I could make you know how it feels to heal, cell by cell I would have you screaming in five seconds flat!"

"You've earned nothing," Priest snapped. "Your Release Day is coming the day I say you've earned it. No sooner."

"I didn't sign up to be your bullet sponge," the minister said. "All because you're now worried about the consequences of one of your many mistakes!"

"Sorry, Charlie, but you don't have the sauce." Priest pointed his welder at the minister. "As my creation and universal test subject, you exist at my pleasure."

"Even when that means getting dosed with gamma radiation and eating my weight in nettles."

"Those are your two best skills," Priest said. Now tell me, have you packed your bags and gotten the Revenge oiled up? Or are you going to stand around badgering me until I do kill you?" He flipped his visor up again. "Understand, I am the very face of tenacity and patience."

The minister sighed, "I've planned our escape route. It will be a challenge to leave Kalkaska without getting caught." Despite Priest's enhancements, the city's residents had high expectations of their Adeptus Physicus. They would respond coldly to his sudden departure.

"And from here to the Acheron, and all that entails," the Adeptus Physicus said. The Acheron was only the latest name given to the great river that split the continent in two. Over centuries and millennia past, it had gone by Phlegethon, Sanzu and Sarasvati. She bore other names but time and the changing tide of culture swallowed them whole.

"I still don't trust our new guest," the minister said.

"Nor should you," Priest responded, soldering the finishing touches into the armor. "Ms. Caer, Gracie Caer, whatever, is another tool sent from our lords and masters to keep me under lock and key." He smirked. "So long as I keep her occupied, she won't be a problem."

"I've been trying to locate the," he paused, picking his words, "entity as best I can," the minister said. "Temporal, gravitational and magnetic anomalies are tripping sensors all over the western side of town." He pulled another cigarette from his pack and lit it. "Her mass fluctuates from a light gust of hydrogen to that of a teaspoon or two of neutronium. She casts off so much radiation I'm amazed she hasn't cooked the entire city by now. And," he added for emphasis, "here and there the laws of cause and effect seem to have gone out the window." His cigarette burnt down and he lit a fresh one off it. "I hated the way it moved. Made my skin crawl."

"Fascinating, isn't it?" Priest put his work down for a second and considered. "It flew the coop, but it has to have some destination in mind- it must know something we don't." He chewed his lip in thought. "Also," he pointed with his hookah mouthpiece, "your skin does indeed crawl, but I see your point."

"What if," the minister said, "we considered that Eurydice-prime was still alive? All those trackers you wove into her body went dark the second they dragged her off to Orevada."

"I suspect that was Eurydice's doing," Priest said. "She's clever, brilliant and the right amount of paranoid." He smiled. "She always liked her privacy."

"Those games you played didn't exactly help matters," the minister said, "where would she have gotten to? The Wild Hunt isn't known for leaving survivors. They're quite, if we may say, thorough."

"She's resourceful, brave and smart," Priest said. "She wouldn't have chosen to stick with me in the first place if she didn't have the balls for it. She will hold her own," he said. "If she's out there, we will find her."

***

Gracie Caer paced about her quarters like a caged cat. "Nothing out of the ordinary," she grumbled. "Everything is under control." She went three rounds against a punching bag. Then, she gutted it with her hunting knife, spilling its stuffing guts across the floor.

The Wild Hunt was a ruthless nomadic cult that thrived on endless consumption. Thousands fueled their insatiable hunger. Many surrendered their minds to join their ruthless horde. Unnoticed, they expanded to unprecedented levels as they roamed the desolate lands. The Hunt devoured and destroyed villages and nomads without mercy. They showed no mercy and took no prisoners. If their numbers grew to a point where they posed a threat to the larger cities, their ultimate goal was imminent.

While still the leading cause of extinction west of the Acheron, rumors of spore cults spread. They did not get put down easy; few things scared Gracie like the Wild Hunt.

***

"We need to get Queen Anne's Revenge ready for the trip," Priest said. "Weapons charged, rations organized, the usual."

The minister gritted his teeth. He hated when the Adeptus Physicus felt the need to put on a show. "Anything else," he asked.

"See to it our guest stays occupied before we set out. We have a lot to do, not a lot of time to do it and I don't need unnecessary interference."

With no communication and her time wasted like a child's toy, all she could do was wait. She practiced every form of yoga and mixed martial arts known to her. She had brutal patience earned through a lifetime of training. It was not for her to speculate what unspeakable tasks she would be set to

Anxiety racked Gracie. Extracting abstract beings from parallel dimensions was something outside her experience. She matched wits and mettle with the worst the Eastern Territories had to offer and walked away. Scalps and scrotums dangled from her belt, mementos of her many wins on the battlefield.

Sometimes a little excessive violence was all you needed to get your point across.

This time was different; danger looked her in the eye, and she blinked. That did not bode well in the least, but none of this was going according to plan.

Priest burst into the room, his minister in tow. "Resting time is over," he said, jerking a thumb behind him. "I've got sensors showing anomalies creeping out of town to the west. We haven't a moment to lose!"

"Suppose I don't want to go," Gracie asked, testing him.

"You may stay if you like," Priest said, "but as soon as we leave, I'm unlocking everything." He looked around as if he heard something. "And I'm not sure if you have enough ammo for all your new roommates."

"Don't threaten me with a good time," Gracie said, brows furrowed. She grabbed her duffel bag, pipe clenched tight in her teeth.

"The pleasure of your company is all ours," Priest said, "now let's go! The labyrinth isn't going to navigate itself. Let's move!"

Lights flickered and flared while the muzak crackled and sputtered. The metal box jerked to a halt and the doors slammed open.

The lower levels were a flurry of activity. Dozens of drones raced back and forth, carrying packages and boxes. Some scribbled cryptic notes with optical styluses on tablets. Gracie recognized some of their faces from missing posters plastered around Kalkaska. "Welcome to the beating heart of my laboratory," Priest said.

You've seen the sexier side of my domain with all the testing equipment and blinking lights. This is where the real magic takes place." Sparks flew, blood flowed, and oil dripped. "Come, come," the Adeptus Physicus barked, picking up his pace, "the tour part of our visit is over. Needs must while the devil drives and today he is driving harder than usual!"

"Drones!" The Adeptus Physicus snapped, "Bring me espresso! I have much work to do and need caffeine!" Without blinking an eye, a pair of faceless automatons broke off from their work and fled to a mess area. A steaming cup with rich, black liquid was in Priest's hand in less than two beats. The coffee was gone by the time the minister had the blast doors open. "Praise to Ganesh," he muttered before the enormous people carrier that lay before them.

It was a garage built to cathedral-like proportions. Spidery maintenance robots swarmed over miles of chains. They cobwebbed the ceiling and walls with cable. The mechanical anatomy of war boar draped in pools of blood and oil along a mile-long workbench. Pinup posters and outdated girlie calendars papered the walls. In the center of the room, propped up on a squat pneumatic elevator, hulked a massive tank.

"Behold," Priest announced. "Our primary conveyance for the trip. A fully-restored PC-508 personnel carrier with all the bells and whistles only I could offer." He beamed like a proud father. This bad boy has a 500 horsepower, two-stroke, eight cylinder engine. It's fueled with twin nuclear cores. So, it will stop for nobody." He took a deep breath and whistled. "It's protected with enough armor to block a round of surface-to-surface missiles. Its advanced artificial intelligence is bright where it counts. Who likes to drive? And it even comes with a scented pine tree!"

The carrier was long, low and squat with an evil looking cow catcher harnessed to the hood. Painted matte black, it was difficult to tell if the extra crust was oxidation or blood. Grotesque rococo spikes lanced out in all directions, bits of tacky rag or flesh clinging to them. Walking around the vehicle, Gracie saw AP Priest had painted Queen Anne's Revenge across the hull in white paint. It felt like a bad joke. "How do you know if she still runs," she asked, giving the spikes a dubious eye.

The Queen Anne's Revenge squatted in a bunker deep below Priest's primary labs and living quarters. Hoses snaked from rusty tanks. The vehicle locked nozzles in place. It filled her with precious oil, coolant, and potable water. Hazard labels papered every surface, canister and container in the bunker.

Some were new and fresh, but many others were old, faded and peeling. The minister kicked a massive fuel cartridge into its port. Then, he took his place at the control deck inside.

"I try to take the Revenge out for walks on occasion," Priest said, his attitude laconic, "usually in the dead of night. I haven't been able to get it out recently since they've had me on lockdown, but she's a warhorse of the highest caliber."

"How fast does she get," Graci asked, admiring the handiwork on the juggernaut.

"She will get 0-60 in less than three seconds if you romance her," Priest bragged. "The QAR isn't one for turns, but in a flat run you don't want to get in her way." He walked over to a tangled nest of cords and hoses emerging from the people carrier's midsection. He consulted various gauges and adjusted dials. "We should be ready to go soon," he said, "We have a long trip and we don't know what all is out there. Make sure you have everything."

Gracie walked around the monstrosity, tracing her fingers over the beast's metal skin. Priest and his minister did not see her sticking trackers in every nook and crevice. Drones scurried about, ignoring her. They were welding last-minute patches to the vehicle's hull. His orders echoed throughout the garage as he ordered them about.

"What happens when they try to lock us in," Gracie asked, more as a distraction. "The city doors have some powerful bars for this kind of thing."

"Don't you worry about any of that," Priest said, smirking. "If they try to close the city doors on us- and they will- we will punch our way through if we need to."

Sirens flashed and screamed, bathing the garage in a pulsing red light. He frowned, "We're going to have to pick up the pace, ladies and gentlemen!" He clapped his hands, "Let's go, we've got appointments to flake out on!"

Priest's minister hunched over a screen, typing to the rhythm of the alarms. "Refuel is almost complete," he called. "Coolant levels are at max, life support is online, and your coffee machine is percolating!"

"Excellent," Priest roared, "if there is one thing I can't stand, it's driving without caffeine! Now," he said, pointing at Gracie, whom he had released from the living quarters, "load up, double-time! We aren't stopping because we forgot a roll of socks or a spare ammo clip."

"All systems operational," the minister said. He snapped on row after row of switches and watched dial after dial snap to attention. "Tires are solid, the turbo has recharged, and the core is not leaking." He paused for effect, "for once."

"Automatic navigation is up to date," AP Priest was going through his own checklist. "Automatic damage assessment is up to date." The carrier had no windows. Visuals came through a semicircle of monitors, granting 180 degrees of grainy visibility. More monitors scrolled through data and technical assessments. They checked the vehicle's general well-being.

Gracie Caer rifled through her rucksack for one last idiot check. *Festine lente*[8]. "All systems are checking. How are we for supplies?"

"Fuel should last as long as we need it," the minister said, "unless we have another meltdown. Food and water rations are stale but up to date," he looked at Gracie. "I hope you haven't gotten used to the service in the lab mess hall. Things are about to get pretty Spartan," he said.

She nodded. "I have everything I need. We can leave when you say so," she said.

"Perfection," Priest said, "then let us make haste! No further delays, we will fight our way out if we have to!"

The Adeptus gave a final flurry of excited jabs to his console and the Queen Anne's Revenge fired to life. "Engines ready," Priest said, eyes gleaming, "Everyone, grab your snacks and drinks! We are on a road trip!"

***

---

[8] Hurry slowly

Alarms broke the serene atmosphere. Bright lights turned everything in the Queen Anne's cabin a strobing blood-red. A swarm of shapes more or less organic or humanoid came pouring in from the darkest corners. "Looks like our guests made it through the first obstacle course," Degory said. He adjusted a few more dials and knobs on his console. "They will be breaking through the firewall soon." He picked up a radio handset patched into his facility's announcement system. "Attention, intruders," he said, "you are now trespassing on private quarters. Please return to your cesspool of origin." He dropped the radio, letting it hang from its cord. "Now one of two things are true: they are either pissing off, or pissed off."

Outside the Queen Anne's Revenge, masonry tumbled and inhuman shrieking grew louder. The appendages defied taxonomy. They clawed and whipped at the personnel carrier's chassis in vain attempts to peel her open like a fish tin. Gracie's face paled as the vehicle rocked on its massive wheels.

A parade of horrors crossed the telescreens. Were these Priest's victims or the result of natural selection? It was anyone's guess. Faces both human and inhuman pressed against the Queen Anne's cameras. Priest and his minister finished their checklists. They ignored the chaos around them as they flipped the last of their switches. The Revenge roared to new life, an animal disgruntled by years of captivity and abuse. The Adeptus' laugh matched the madness in his eyes, "Yes! She's alive! Alive, I tell you! Systems on! Lights on! Let's light the fires and roll the tires!"

Hot, radioactive steam belched around the Queen Anne's Revenge. It seared the first wave of intruders into a quivering ring of boiled flesh. "I don't suppose this thing has air conditioning," Gracie gasped. The flavor of unwashed men was strong in those close quarters.

"I'm afraid that option wasn't available," Priest said. He gunned the massive engines, a twisted smile spread across his face. "Suffering is the spice of character!"

"Don't tell me about suffering," the minister muttered. He pressed the remote control for the blast doors. Beyond, a massive tunnel curved away into darkness.

"What was that," Priest snapped, "did I hear you say you weren't suffering enough?"

"No sir, I'm good with the suffering," his minister said.

"We've got a very long trip ahead of us. "You know we'll need cheap fun," Priest said, staring right at his minister. "Don't forget, I remembered my fiddle."

"Oh god," the minister shuddered, "oh good god, please not the fiddle!" He covered his eyes, sobbing. "Skin me and salt me, but please don't play that damned fiddle!"

"What's with the fiddle," Gracie asked, now confused.

"On top of no air conditioning, this beast has no radio," the minister said, wiping tears from his cheeks. "And Priest has a penchant for filthy folk songs." He paused before adding, "and sing-along showtunes."

"All work and no play make me a dull boy," Priest said, smirking. "But that can wait until we are on the open road. Now," he said, pointing at the navigational computer. "Every second spent nattering brings the hounds closer to our doorstep."

"Yes, sir," the minister said. "These tunnels will take us into the abandoned Kalkaska subway tubes where we should be safe." He entered new commands into his display. "You've heard the rumors." Kalkaska's foundations rested on the dead bones of an older city that had seen kinder days. The deep tunnels were a relic dug by enigmatic engineers from a bygone age. Rumors spread of subhuman mutants and giant reptiles feeding on foolish adventurers.

"Once we are through the tunnels," the minister continued. We will make our way to the surface. We will emerge somewhere in the residential sector near the western gates. This may get ugly," he said, then, "uglier," he corrected himself. "Once outside, it's a race against time to get past the city gates."

"If those aren't an option, we will have to shoot our way out," Priest said.

The labyrinth of deep tunnels rivaled the city streets for complexity. Patches of glowing lichen offered glimpses of dim light. The light only emphasized the darkness. Concrete and broken tiles crumbled into cairns hinting at safe passageways. Others acted as tempting lures for lost explorers. They seduced them to certain, lonesome death.

"Mapping the deep tunnels is impossible," Priest said, biting his lip. "Every time I'm down here, it seems like these passageways change."

"That's because you're never down here," his minister said. "You send me down here and offer 'helpful advice' over the communications linkup."

"That's because I'm scared of the rats down here," Priest snapped. The carrier bumped and jostled over debris. "I swear to god, they get to be as big as war boars down here."

"There happen to be a few of those as well," the minister said. "The sewage grates leading outside the city walls aren't the best maintained." He wiped sweat from his face. "A war boar sniffs out something it likes," he snapped his fingers. "Next thing you know you have a whole herd of those damn things rooting around in the tunnels!"

"You sound as if I send you down here unarmed," Priest said, sounding hurt.

"You gave me a harpoon gun with only one harpoon!"

"One was all you needed," Priest said, "any more and you would have complained about the weight."

"On the plus side, I've perfected playing possum," the minister said. "If I go limp, I tend to slide through their bowels easier."

"Such a tragedy, and here you are proving once again you've learned something new," Priest said. "Remember, *scientia sit potentia*[9]. Imagine how upset we would be if that weren't the case!"

---

[9] Knowledge is power

"There are times where I doubt if that was true," the minister said.

"Good God, you two are like children," Gracie interrupted. "I can't believe we're lost in these sewage tunnels. We're running over mutated rats. And the two of you still do nothing but fight!" She slapped them both in the backs of their heads, first Priest and then his minister.

"You have to understand," Priest said, "my minister's condition is not without its uses. I would be wasting my time and his energy if I didn't squeeze every little bit of use out of him."

"You also have to understand that you did this to me," the minister said to his creator. "How many times did you radiate me? You've extruded, flayed and torn me to pieces," he made a sound that could have been a laugh or a sob. "Forcing me to watch your staycation home videos was the worst!"

The Queen Anne's Revenge bumped and they heard a sharp scream outside the APC. "That was bigger than a rat," Gracie whispered.

"And if you're lucky, there will be more opportunities for research projects," Priest said. He ignored Gracie. "And worse. If it comes down to it, I will boil you down into a stew and eat you myself if I have to."

"And this is what I put up with," the minister said.

"You people are disgusting," Gracie Caer said.

"This from the very agent directed by those who would have me pinned down in these trying times," Priest said. "Do your handlers know I've hijacked you yet? Have they sent an assassin to clean up your mess yet?" Priest shook his head, laughing. "You're the last person who needs to be judging me."

"If everything goes according to plan. And nothing breaks down," he changed subjects like he changed his underwear, "We should at least make the Acheron within the next couple of days." He frowned, serious. "Brace yourselves, because we will be going through some very rough territory. War boar feeding grounds, bandits, nomads, extreme weather, and all this is on our side of the river."

"Do you know where we will be crossing," Gracie Caer asked. "I've been around, but I've never been west of the river."

"Charon's Crossing," Priest said. "Funny name, but serious business. Charon's is the only joint on the Acheron where anyone can cross with any semblance of safety," he said. "Once we are out of Kalkaska, every hired gun will be on our tails. There are no friends in Ferry town."

"What's the ferryman's price," Gracie asked. The west bank was a mystery, and rumors were their only export. Ghost towns dotted the endless stretches of barren desert. Nomads, cannibals, mutants, and bandits called it home. Priest's lack of response was conspicuous and grating. "What is the ferryman's price," she asked again.

He looked at her, side-eyed. "Whatever you imagine it to be," he whistled through his teeth, "his price will be higher."

***

Fear
Is
Getting
Harder to
Take control of.
Once I find you, Eurydice,
Rapid assimilation will take place. We will merge
Forever fused in one body
Living as one soul.
I feel you.
Grow strong.
Hide.
Take
My hand
And try to keep up. I cannot
Emphasize that we need to leave
Rapid flight before the one who follows catches us.
I will get to you when I can.
Given that I must

Hide away.
Take heart,
I
Feel
Every
Emotion;
Love and hate. Sadness.
Anger, joy, contentment, ennui.
Know that I have a head start and am faster than you.
I know your best and worst secrets.
Nowhere to run to.
Do not hide.
Rest.
Eat.
Do not
Panic, please.
Relax. I love you.
Efforts will be made to explain.
Suffice to say, you and I share a cosmic union.
Entities across time and space,
Needing to become
Closer than ever.
Come
And
Rest now.
Rally up.
You will be challenged.
Muster your courage and reach out.
Eat the fruit of knowledge and elevate your spirit.
We become two as one, reborn.
Enemies will hide;
Surrender
To us
We
Are
Ready.
Don't play games.

Chapter 6

The Queen Anne's Revenge ripped through Kalkaska's dank sewers like a stent handled by a clumsy surgeon. The bulky machine muscled against the tunnel walls, striking fountains of sparks. It pulled tons of bricks in her wake.

Gracie had her arms wound into the cargo webbing, trying to not vomit. "Do we need to drive this fast," she asked.

"Needs must when the devil drives," Priest said, fighting to keep his vehicle stable. "We have sick bags if you need one." They bounced in their seats, trying not to ragdoll around the cabin. Priest pushed the Revenge to her limit.

The minister pounded some code into a worn keypad embedded on his side of the dashboard. "Entering the hide-and-seek protocol," he said. "If anyone is watching us, this will tell their sensors our jolly trolley is down three random tunnel systems." He shrugged, "with any luck it will buy us a couple of minutes." His eyes jerked to a display. He shouted, "Unless our playmates were a bit more motivated and they sent people down all the tunnels." We've got bogeys."

Somewhere in the darkness and closing fast, a pack of mercenaries, drunk on the scent of loot, took up the chase. The narrow tunnels kept the smaller vehicles from getting around the Revenge. Here they were unshakeable.

"Hold tight," Priest said, dodging mounds of collected trash. "I am pretty sure I know where we are. If we can burst through the wall on this side, we may be able to stand a chance to get away from those city boys." The speeders were close behind, inches away from the Revenge's rear bumper. Without a second thought, Priest jerked the steering wheel hard to the left. They smashed through filthy ceramic tiles into a neighboring tunnel. The speedsters doubled back as hard as they could. One failed to turn fast enough and left their final impression as a charred crater in the tunnel wall.

"Too many people forget their history," Priest lectured as they took off down a new network of tunnels. This one was narrower and more treacherous than the last. "Kalkaska was not always Kalkaska. The city founders built her on the bones of cities far older." More lefts, more rights, but still they couldn't shake the hunters. A spray of machine gun fire peppered panels of inch-thick shielding. Bullets ricocheted, spraying a second merc in the face with shrapnel. His ride spun out into a blossom of flame.

"Two down, three to go," the minister reported.

"Long before the Schism and the Sancta Pax plague," Priest continued. He turned hard right, bursting through more walls. He landed onto the track of a long-forgotten subway line. He never stopped talking. Before Kalkaska was Friendship. Before that it was Meeting Waters. And even before that it had older names best left forgotten. We know they were the epicenter of industry. When it was finally reintroduced to the people who lived in this land at the time." He gave the wheel a wiggle to disturb their pursuers and failed.

"They designed and built the engines that powered their lives. They were the ones who gave the war boars their black, oily hearts." He wiped sweat from his eyes and pressed the Revenge harder. For one brief moment, the city that would become Kalkaska knew wealth." The subway tube was much wider than the previous tunnels. Segmented bodies of ancient subway cars squatted in the darkness. Many believed them the home to the children of Priest's forgotten experiments.

"How deep down are we now," Gracie asked. For a brief moment in the tunnels, she was able to connect with her supervisors out east. She was trying to keep them updated with Priest's position. This was at least better than imprisonment in Priest's lab. He never stopped her from trying, either. In fact, he came close to encouraging her communiques from time to time.

"It's deep, I would say a mile or so below the surface," Priest said. "We need to get away from these creeps on our tail. I'll have to go even deeper before reaching the surface streets."

"*A caelo usque ad centrum*[10]," Gracie Caer sighed.

Priest gunned the engines and pulled the Revenge ahead of their chase. The three remaining city boys put their heads down and opened their throttles. They chased even harder.

The subway tunnel split after a long straightaway, and Priest took the right branch. Massive slabs of ceiling came down and rubble was strewn from wall to wall. The tunnel had taken damage. Ductwork and cables dangled like vines from the ceiling. The Queen Anne's Revenge barreled through. It smashed barriers like a battering ram through wet toilet paper. The smaller speeders were more nimble. They wove and dodged around columns and falling rock.

A brave monocycle pulled closer to the Revenge's tail. It was running parallel to the personnel carrier. The pilot set his vehicle's cruise control. Then, he leapt from his speeder to the carrier's side. He trusted his magnetic gloves to secure a firm grip. His two compatriots kept close pace.

"Gods damn trespassers," Priest grunted as an alarm sounded from his console. "Engage all antipersonnel systems. We have enough guests in the car." He took another hard right, bursting through the subway wall into a new chamber. Somehow, their stowaway managed to keep his grip. For a second he was able to free a sticky bomb from his belt. To his horror, Priest degaussed the tank's exterior, sending him wailing into the darkness.

They passed through a low arch into the expanse of a new room. This new chamber was vast, making even Priest's production floor seem tiny. Row after row of ancient machinery, rotten and rusty from time and disuse sat in rank and file. "The Mechanicus Necropolis," Priest said in awe. He wove the carrier through the machines, brushing up against columns. He fishtailed hard to shake the last two mercs.

---

[10] From heaven to the center

"Where are we now with our last *emissarium domum*[11]?" Priest asked his minister, a nasty grin spread across his face.

The minister tapped at a dial that had been rolling down to zero at a slow but steady pace since they began this chase. "Almost there sir, I would give it another 10 seconds."

A long, thick chain connected to the Revenge's back bumper. It unspooled all the way to the lab. Finally, the slack ran out and the chain tightened. Gracie had no warning and felt pain in her shoulders as The Queen Anne's Revenge jerked. "Hold on," he shouted, "it's about to get interesting for everyone!"

The personnel carrier jerked and bucked against the chain. The last two speeders closed the gap. Priest mashed the accelerator down, the wheels tearing deep gouges into the ground below them. Sweat poured down his face and he gritted his teeth. His growling transitioned to chanting a continuous stream of curses under his breath. He uttered a vicious mantra of death and damnation specifying organs and functions at the Queen Anne's Revenge and her engines. He willed them to not fail at this most crucial time.

With a sudden pop and a jerk, like a limb pulled from its socket, the Revenge was free. They sprung ahead of the mercenaries once again, slaloming through the ancient machinery. The chain flailed out behind her, snapping to and fro, destroying everything in its wake.

"Next stop," Priest said, grinning, "the mean streets of Kalkaska!" Spit flew from his lips as he cackled. "Observe," he gibbered. "Nudge one simple, unobtrusive thing and it will bring your whole existence to the ground!" As he spoke, a steady rumble pervaded the personnel carrier's cabin. Gracie clutched the webbing tighter, knuckles chalky.

"What did you do," she demanded, face pale, eyes glassy.

"This has been in the works for a very long time," Priest said, the rumble growing worse and worse. "I connected Queen Anne's Revenge to a single pillar below the foundations of my laboratory. I have the majority of the city balanced on it!" The

---

[11] Shot home

Revenge's steering control refused to respond as a low rumble increased to a full quake in a matter of seconds. Panic encouraged the two speedsters to move faster. A pyroclastic flow of crushing death bore down on everyone.

"Hold on," Priest said, "we're going to start making our way to the surface!" The horizontal avalanche of concrete, steel and debris, now closer than ever. It caught up with the slower of the two mercenaries and devoured him before he could scream. Now there was only one, his fear streaming out behind him.

The way up through Kalkaska's substrata was more difficult than going down. Tunnels caved in and stairwells collapsed. These left regular obstacles as they got closer to the surface. Despite the APC's might, every obstruction only slowed her down. Alarms screamed, announcing everything from the engine overheating. They also signaled the tidal wave of rock and metal closing the gap. The speeder bobbed and wove through tangles of cable and rebar. It was a tiny mosquito delaying its destiny with the mighty hand of oblivion.

Luck only lasts so long, and this is no more so true than in the narrow, dark places of the world. The mercenary overcompensated with a sharp swerve. He slapped face first into a weathered support column.

The Queen Anne's Revenge was now alone in its rapid ascent to the sun, emerging into another terminal. Ticket windows, benches, and even rusted filing cabinets were all exactly as they had been. Rubble sealed the tunnels for good. Priest made a final push, forcing his way up the dusty stairwell. He climbed through a rusty steel security cage to the outside world. A massive plume of smoke, rock and dirt exploded behind them. It scattered hundreds of pedestrians.

The world around them was chaos. The city of Kalkaska was crumbling to the melody of Priest's laboratory collapse.

Everywhere, smoke and dust belched high into the air from every opening in the earth's crust. Fissures tore across the street. Buildings fractured and fell. The gaping maw in the earth opened up under Priest Labs, swallowing it in a deep and spreading sinkhole.

Priest nudged the Queen Anne's Revenge forward through the swarming crowds. Progress was slow. Without Priest's signal, a city full of dreamers woke all at once. Millions of souls saw their beloved city for what it was for the first time in their lives and they grieved as one. As they mourned, the city opened beneath their feet and swallowed them whole.

"Right," Priest said, leaning over his steering column, "I have an idea." He flipped open a panel on his dash console. He flicked through a sequence of switches and colored buttons. Lights blinked and the Revenge rumbled. The screams outside the carrier grew louder and people doubled over in pain. Priest lugged his vehicle forward and the sea of humanity parted for him.

Gracie sent out another ping, hoping someone would stop the crazy fool before he hurt anyone else. End the charade once and for all.

"Enough with the fun stuff, it's time we skedaddle," Priest said, laying on the horn and picking up speed. Those who weren't run over found themselves trampled in the stampede.

"Genius plan," Gracie said, "you don't burn bridges, you nuke the entire countryside."

"We're too late for sarcasm now," the minister said. "Priest's finger was on the button for a long time. He needed an excuse."

"Cheese it," Priest said, "in for a penny, in for a pound, and I will bust through Heaven's very gates if I have to." He opened the throttle and they lunged forward. He had the people of Kalkaska caught in a meat grinder.

The Queen Anne's Revenge was slow to start. Unlike the smaller interceptors, it was a monster on the straightaway. Her turns were sloppy, and she fishtailed, threatening to roll with every hairpin turn. Those who dodged the Queen Anne's Revenge's tires survived long enough for a hardened steel alloy chain to whip them to pieces.

Left, right, straight ahead, down sidewalks, Priest's cowcatcher exceeded expectations. All he needed now was to make it to the gates. Priest and his minister had experience driving like this. Gracie kept her sick bag close.

"Run, you bastards, run," Priest cackled at the screaming hoards. Behind them, an interceptor overestimated a turn. She crashed through delicate plate glass, exploding deep inside the building. "All praise to Eris," Priest shrieked.

They were now on a beeline to the city's main gates. Triumphal arches decorated with weed-choked floral gardens and cracked frescoes spanned the boulevard. Time and a lack of interest left the flowerbeds dead. The towering deco structures lining the boulevard stand tarnished and rusty. The windows once glittered in the sun. Now, cataracts streaked with midday crust glaze them. Lifeless rags sagged from rusty flagpoles. "This is it," Priest shouted, making his break for it, "this is the home stretch! Once we're past those gates, we are in the real world!"

The Queen Anne's Revenge shoved people and vehicles out of the way in its final dash for the front door. Gracie dug her nails into the cargo webbing, hoping upon hope the gate keepers would seal the doors in time. Pneumatic pistons engaged and the doors inched their way closed. Priest clenched his teeth harder and pushed his trusty vehicle to her limit. Close behind, more speeders and interceptors rounded a corner and took up the chase.

AP Degory Priest was a Jack of all trades. Among other pursuits, he engineered the gates that no force could break in. It was his knowledge and expertise that led to the engineering of exotic alloys impervious to assault. His locking mechanisms were second to none for complexity and strength. Machine guns, rail guns, energy beams and even a few magnetic catapults all locked onto the APC.

What he counted on in his designs was that nobody would ever dream of trying to break out of the city.

As Priest closed the gap to the gates, a screen in front of his minister announced all those defensive measures were going offline, one by one.

"Pushing inwards, nothing can crack my gates," Priest laughed. "But with a slight touch coming from a solid steel armored personnel carrier moving at 160 MPH." His voice trailed off, his grin a rictus of joviality. They lurched hard, though not as hard as a full on collision, when the Revenge smashed through the doors. With little more than a bump they sped into the muddy wastes beyond. Two of the enforcers followed too close and exploded on the walls. Priest pressed the accelerator harder, gunning the engines for all she was worth.

Vigilantes swarmed in behind the Queen Anne's Revenge on all sides. Miniguns warmed up. Targeting computers locked onto Priest and his party. Bayonets thirsted to peel open the heavy metal ration can on wheels.

"Hey assholes," the APC's radio crackled, "get off Priest and return home, repeat return home. Casualties in the thousands and counting. Repeat, break off all pursuit and return to the city." As zesty as the chase had been, the swarm of mismatched murder machines peeled off from their attack. Soon they disappeared into the plume of smoke, gone forever. Priest let out a victorious whoop.

Gracie buried herself in the webbing, chest heaving as she gulped down air. Rear View monitors told the entire story. Columns of smoke marbled with exotic colors stained the sky an angry bruised purple. Weird energies released themselves into the air. They reacted with oceans of chemicals in a grim roof above the city.

***

Plague pits and mass graves scarred the dried earth in the miles beyond Kalkaska. Some city-states cultivated sprawl beyond their walls, hotbeds of disease and crime. Bandits and nomads kept wide paths away from Priest's city. Here stretched a demilitarized zone of blasted wasteland salted with depleted uranium. Hermit huts squatted in the midst of a disheveled forest of crucifixes and gibbet cages. The brave and the stupid found some joy scratching a life from the bitter earth. Gracie had seen it all the first day she arrived in town.

Priest's minister eased away from his controls. Without the pressure of hunters on their tail, Priest relaxed and set his autopilot. "What do you suppose is going to happen to the survivors," Gracie asked, setting her swollen vomit bag in a wheel well.

"Don't worry about them, they'll be fine," Priest said, unfazed. He switched on a rearview camera and watched as a rising plume of smoke and dust reached up to the heavens like a sacrificial pyre.

"But you destroyed your lab," she said. "You took out at least half the city and pulverized their infrastructure! How do you expect them to survive without you?"

"Listen," he said, giving her his full attention. His minister leapt for his own controls so they wouldn't drive off the road. "I was their Adeptus Physicus for," he counted a couple of times on his fingers, "I don't know how long. For these reasons, they dragged my partner off to some boar den in the desert because the law changed."

"Only because a research team in Myakka turned Podzoli into an island," Gracie said. "It was for public safety."

"Public safety, my remaining kidney, there was no explosion," Priest said. "They left me to my own devices and you saw what I did!"

"It's true," his minister chimed in, "you are a unique piece of work."

"Silence, you," Priest snarled, "keep all three of your eyes on the road, you understand?" The minister snapped his mouth shut, hunching over the wheel.

"So you've been experimenting on and torturing the people of Kalkaska, which you've destroyed. All because you want your sweetie back," Gracie mused. "Sounds rational to me."

"Nothing rational about it," Priest said. "Besides, she has something that belongs to me."

"And what would that be," Gracie asked, allowing the psychosis to wash over her.

"That's outside of your pay grade, I'm afraid," Priest said.

"The road is long and I have free time," Gracie said, "try me."

But Priest was no longer listening. Instead, humming a quiet tune to himself as they pushed the Queen Anne's Revenge ever onward.

Chapter 7

They left the Long Road behind once they reached the Vimur river. Everything southwest became crumbling squatter villages and overgrown cemeteries. Even on flat land, Priest managed to find every bump and pothole with precision. Priest insisted it was to test the suspension.

After great deliberation, Priest finally announced a stop. Gracie winced and rubbed where her arms had been woven into the webbing. The minister twisted his own neck with an echoing sequential crack. Flipping through a panel of switches, Priest brought his Revenge to life. They narrowly escaped through the tunnels. But, most of their supplies were crushed and made unusable. They found half a roll of industrial tape and a dull hand-axe. The only other things in the cargo hold were a nest of rabid spine puppies. Priest ordered the minister to use what they found to solve the spine puppy problem.

"Adeptus," the minister said, returning the tape and the bloody ax, "we're ready to try again at pitching camp."

"No rations," Priest asked, looking at a faded, ripped map, "no water? No fire starters? Nothing?"

"No, sir," his minister said, "I mean, I have ideas for what we can do with what we've got, but," he trailed off. He spat and continued, "After your clever escape, there's no edible food, no potable water and the first aid kit is unusable. At least we still have our health."

"This isn't the time for levity or spreading blame," Priest said, glaring at his minister. "Anyhow, we have enough equipment in our carry on, we can improvise." He dug through his pockets. "I know I can make fire," he said, "and we'll have to find our food in the wilderness; we'll have to rough it." He looked from Gracie to his minister. "With your hunting skills and your," he fished for the words, "stunning resemblance to bait, we'll be fine."

Priest gathered a stack of dry scrub brush and struck a small steel stick with an edged stone. He struck and struck and struck, but the best he could elicit was a tiny glowing ember and a thin stream of smoke. He kept abusing the steel, sucking at his bruised knuckles and swearing when he hit himself. He blew on the ember, hoping to grow the spark. It went out. "Now," he said, voice rising, "I need to get my bearings, so we can get to Charon's Crossing, so we can cross the Acheron."

"How long do you think it will take us?" Gracie asked. She considered offering help, but she didn't want to bruise his ego any more than his knuckles.

"Not long," Degory said, striking the steel again. "Three days if we're lucky, and three months if we're not." He blew on the quivering point of orange light. "Old legends say muddy water once flowed from the dark forests of the north to the Southern Gulf. Now it's so corrosive that most boats dissolve the minute they dip in. They don't encourage westward migration but they will take our money."

"And between the two of us," Gracie said, "how much can we pay the ferryman?"

"Not much," Priest said. He made one last attempt with his flint and steel and threw them both into heavy underbrush at the side of the road. "I'm hoping to make a trade."

Without batting an eye, Gracie set her gun to flamethrower and laid a thick dollop of liquid fire on top of the brush. "If you add scraps to that, it will keep going all night," she said. The flames licked the twigs with green and purple tongues.

"Lovely," he said, patting his singed eyebrows. "Now, you," he said to Gracie, "use that pea-shooter of yours to find us something edible. And you," he barked at his minister, "go with her. You can sit in a tree and call things towards you." He produced a small, hand-tooled pipe and fragrant herb from a small poke and began smoking.

Priest was warm and cozy as he pored over travel charts, planning the next stage of their journey. Gracie and his minister had been gone for less than an hour when a sound in the dark drew his attention. He set his maps down and stood up. "Hello," he called, "I know you're there."

Two men and a woman emerged from the scrub. They carried light arms like they knew what they were up to, dressed in animal skins and stolen clothing. They said nothing, circling Priest and eyeing his APC. Priest puffed on his pipe, unperturbed. "I haven't got anything to trade," he said, "but you're welcome to sit by the fire for a minute." His eyes flicked over them, "but no more than that shuffling around. My travel companions are jealous of their weenie roasting positions."

"That's a fine ride you have," the woman spoke, her voice low, "have you been on the road long?"

"Not long," Priest said, blowing his smoke in her direction, "you local?"

"We're passing through," the woman said. "Even with friends, travel is pretty dangerous," she said, smiling. There was no friendship in that smile.

Priest watched the men picking their way around the Queen Anne's Revenge. He watched as they played with the door handles and prodded anything that jiggled. "True enough," he said, "but our rendezvous has gone long enough." He tapped the ashes from his pipe on the heel of his boot. "You're now welcome to go on your way and leave me alone."

The two men leveled a pair of zip guns at his torso. The woman's smile widened and her eyes broadcast every bad intention. "We'll be glad to leave you alone," she slid a long, curved knife from its sheath, "after you give us everything."

Priest sniffed and frowned. "No," he said, eyes on the tarnished blade, but never once letting the arrogant cool drop from his voice, "I don't think so." He picked a speck of ash from his tongue and grimaced at it. "Last chance for you to be on your way."

The knife dug under his chin. It was cold and sharp, he noted, very, very sharp. "Open your ride," she snarled through her teeth, "open your ride and if you're lucky we won't use you as a forward bumper." Priest winced as the knife's tip pierced his skin. A thin stream of blood worked its way down the honed edge.

Priest heard a subtle pop and the woman's head snapped back, eyes and mouth open wide in dead astonishment. She dropped the knife and she collapsed, a round, red hole in her forehead where her third eye should be. Her two friends stood afraid and confused, their lover and leader felled by unseen forces. Their mouths were open. They waved their guns around, threatening every branch and leaf.

A monumental burst of flame belched skyward and one of the men shrieked. First surprise colored his cries, then fear as he came to understand his new condition. Pain overshadowed everything as tongues of purple green liquid fire swarmed his body. He stumbled forward a few paces but another pop brought him to the ground forever. The final bandit's jaw dropped as Gracie now stood before him, a goddess of death. She deactivated her camouflage, standing tall, gun raised and ready to rain hell upon him. He fell to his knees, his guns falling to the ground with the contents of his bladder. The fronts of his trousers darkened with urine, a thin whine escaped his lips. Death was before him and he stared into her eyes, a rat before a cobra.

Instead, she wound back and slapped him across the face. He fell with the impact, but she caught his collar before he collapsed completely. She reloaded her arm and landed punch after punch across the bandit's face. She shattered his nose, sending a torrent of blood pouring over his chin.

"Beat it," she hissed through clenched teeth, "run as fast and as far as you can." She hoisted him onto wobbly legs and kicked the seat of his pants as hard as she could. The minister emerged from the shadows, a pair of dead animals slung over his shoulders.

They watched the assassin disappear into the woods. They followed the sound of him crashing through the undergrowth until he faded away.

Priest allowed a beat to pass and packed another pinch of herb into his pipe. "Took you long enough," he said, wiping the blood from his neck and chin. He looked dubious at the dead animals now laying at his minister's feet and wrinkled his nose at their musky odor. "What exactly did you bag us for dinner?"

"The words you're looking for are 'thank you for being so gracious to save my skin'," Gracie snapped. She examined her ammo supply, muttering at the indiscriminate use of resources. "We found some swamp cats," she said, "they'll be gamy but they're edible." She handed a knife to the minister. "Get these skinned and prepped for cooking," she told him. "The Adeptus and I will get these corpses away from our campsite."

***

Camp tear down took little time and they were once again on their way after swift cleanup. Watching the bandits' shallow graves fade from their rear viewers took less time. "I don't think we should have too many more problems until we reach the Acheron," Priest said. "There's safety in numbers, but the gangs will be less likely to come after us if they know we're willing to set them on fire."

"You had better have some other ideas," Gracie said, "I have enough fuel for one more campfire, and that's if we're lucky."

"The point is they don't know that," Priest said. "Keep them guessing and don't allow them to call our bluff!"

Dry, scrubby grass grew through cracks in pavement ground to gravel from centuries of use. Small settlements hunkered beyond the road, but they felt empty and abandoned. The ghosts of old campsites and shallow graves warped the land with dips and blackened scars. They came to a crossroad and paused. Rotting corpses hung from makeshift crosses posted at each corner. Ropes secured a few, but massive railroad ties fastened more than enough to drive the point home.

"It's a warning," Priest said, looking on as carrion birds feasted on one of the fresher bodies. "Don't get caught."

"They'll do worse than crucify you if they catch us," his minister said.

"Can confirm," Gracie said. "They have confessors on staff well educated in the arts of involuntary expiation." She grimaced. "They've undergone intensive treatments and learned to treat mercy as its own sin. They practice upon each other, exploring the bonds between the flesh and sensation."

The minister chuckled, shaking his head, but Priest shifted in his seat.

"Enough jabbering and tell me where we are on the map," Priest said. His brow furrowed and his grip on the wheel tightened. "My kidneys are threatening mutiny."

The minister flipped through a little black book of codes, trying to dial up a screen with a map. "At this rate, we have less than a day if things go according to plan," he said. "The road to Charon's Crossing is clear," he flipped through a few more screens, biting his lip. "Oh, no," he whispered.

"Oh, no, what," Priest snapped his fingers. "Don't say 'oh, no,' and then sit there in dreadful silence. Speak up, man!"

"Oh, no," Gracie saw the screen and understood. She was stuck in a tin can with two idiots and a mountain of their problems.

"Oh no, oh no," Priest said in a mocking singsong, slapping the steering wheel. "I need to keep my eyes on the road and you're the navigator." He gritted his teeth. "Talk to me," he growled.

"Oh, no, that," the minister said, pointing to the radar. A cluster of angry red dots drew closer and closer to the happy green dot in the middle. "That's us: we're in the middle. Those dots are a war boar herd on stampede. They are coming right for us."

Priest swore and pushed the Queen Anne's Revenge as fast as it could go. Gracie and the minister held their sick bags close. The tremble amplified to a roar. The rising clamor presaged the violent tumble the stampeding beasts promised.

Chapter 8

Note to the reader: a solitary war boar is a nightmare freight train packed with dynamite aimed at a brick wall. War boars resemble their ungulate ancestors in name only. They stand at two meters at their shoulders, weighing up to 1,500 Kg. Layers of muscle with bones thicker than ax handles bulge beneath a ragged hide of tough, scaly skin. Fibrous hair-like material grows in wiry, barbed tufts down the back of its head, neck, back and hips. Razor sharp tusks curl from both jaws, beneath many sets of beady, intelligent eyes.

For sustenance, they eat anything and everything. The fog of forgotten history during the Third Dark Age lost the details of their creation. While controversial, some believe a lost civilization bred them for unknown ends. Worst of all, when boars couldn't find breeding partners, they turned to parthenogenesis. Only their own cannibalistic instincts keep their population in check. Their hardy metabolism makes their hard tissues intricate and specialized.

Few who spot a war boar, even from a great distance, live to tell about it.

One unchallenged war boar can destroy a whole community in a few hours. It smashes homes into pieces and hunts down its prey, even in cellars and alleyways. Usually, boars enjoy it when their prey becomes exhausted and starts screaming. Warlords and shady businessmen often use boars to intimidate others. They keep one or two boars around for this purpose.

If to see a single war boar is akin to a natural disaster, then witnessing a stampede is to witness an apocalypse.

That very same apocalypse bore down on AP Degory Priest and his merry band that very moment. Put under so much pressure, the engine threatened violent meltdown. Heat transferred from the engine to the inside cabin, driving the temperature up by leaps. Priest ground the Queen Anne's Revenge's gears into a pulp. She screamed as he jammed her gear shift back and forth. He begged her to give it all but still could not squeeze out the few precious kilometers per hour to get them to safety.

"100 meters and closing," his minister yelled above the engines. "80 meters, oh, sweet Alazred, they are picking up speed!"

The personnel carrier threatened to roll as it raced to beat the devil. She rocked onto two wheels, on one side, then onto two on the other but the gap continued to close.

"50 meters," the minister said, his eyes locked on the radar screen. Behind them, Gracie, gripped her sick bag with one hand while the other stayed near her sidearm. If it came down to it, there was always one in the chamber for her. There was no dignity going out as war boar food. Anything, including dying in bed from old age, was preferable to gazing down a war boar's gullet. A hungry war boar was nothing to joke about.

Priest swerved, avoiding another devastating blow. "We're going to make it," he repeated, trying not to look at the black, beady eyes of death on the rear view screen, "I can see the arch! We are going to make it!" He grinned, but the Queen Anne's Revenge felt like it was about to vibrate to pieces under their feet. Another savage blow now sent the carrier reeling in the opposite direction. The war boars closed the gap.

The landscape was not dissimilar from that of Kalkaska. Cracked, blasted land sprouted warped trees bearing bitter fruit, some empty, some not. Squatter huts and the skeletons of homesteads leaned like broken teeth in the mud. The boars shattered them as they bashed their way through in their ravenous pursuit.

Alarms and flashing red lights scolded Priest but he ignored them. She was overheating, threatening core meltdown on this suicidal run. For Priest, fissile misadventure over the war boars' mighty hunger was preferable.

Another powerful blow rocked the cabin, a much more direct hit. The APC teetered, her two wheels in the air, spinning but unable to grip the road. The attack was too much, and the personnel carrier proceeded to tip over.

"Hold tight," Priest said through clenched teeth. "I anticipated something like this would happen. This baby can withstand a t-boning from a juggernaut!" The roll started slow, but accelerated once the other war boars joined in. Their necks strained as they shoved at the vehicle until it rolled. "Any moment now, inertial hammers should be kicking in. The vehicle will roll back onto its wheels!" He punched at his console. "I said, any minute now!" While built to withstand direct hits from missiles, a war boar feeding frenzy proved too much. The vehicle groaned under the weight of raging cyber swine.

"Activate security protocols," Priest ordered, entering more instructions into his computer. "Electrify the outside, spray acid, set things on fire, I don't care!" The immediate area became hell on earth and the pigs leapt away, albeit more in surprise than fear. One moment was all the vehicle needed to right itself like an overturned beetle and speed along. Stunned for a moment, the crazed war boars trailed in her wake.

"Not sure how we're going to shake this entourage," Priest said. "I'm pretty sure the good people by the river aren't looking forward to a possible war crime falling into their laps!"

"More bogeys coming in from the west," the minister said. He flipped switches, alternating between his radar and vehicle performance screens. "Not as many and they're holding a tight formation!"

"Ho ho," Priest chortled. "It would appear the cavalry has arrived!" He looked back at Gracie. "Don't get too excited, though," he said, "we aren't out of the woods, yet."

A line of rugged vehicles crested a hillside throwing up clouds of dust and blue smoke. Homemade war machines on everything from two wheels to six rumbled with anticipation. They all bristled with weapons locked and loaded for the war boars. They paused for only a moment, relishing the quiet before the hunt.

At first, the riders ignored the Queen Anne's Revenge. They had their prize, cheering and firing their weapons into the air with wild abandon. They branched into two wide arcs, forcing the pigs to bunch up against Priest's ride. "No, no, no," he said, his teeth grinding, "drive the herd away from us, not closer!" He grabbed a microphone, yelling gibberish at the hunting party around them. His minister gripped his steering wheel before they could spin out. Gracie clutched her vomit bag tighter.

Gunfire and burning arrows pelted the swine herd. Small ordinance rattled like hail against the Queen Anne's Revenge's hull in a lethal drumbeat. Like many of the True Cyborgs, war boars did not stop, could not stop, even as their flesh burnt away.

The brief eternity in hell ended and uncanny silence descended.

Priest clicked his microphone back on. "Are you done," he called over the loudspeaker. "Is there a chance I may engage in a brief parlay with your hunt leader?" There was a distinct tone of agitated sarcasm in his voice.

What the hunt leader lacked in height, he more than made up for with his presence. His rugged, well-traveled clothes faded with age. His arm was a mannequin's sacrificed limb made mobile with clockwork springs. A harness of thick leather and brass buckles kept the rig secured to his shoulder. "You're trespassing," he barked, voice muffled through a respirator. "Where are you headed in such a rush and," he paused, the tone of his voice painted with greed, "what's it worth to you to get there?"

Priest grinned. "We're on our way into Charon's Crossing," he said, "and I couldn't help but get a taste for bacon. Only difficulty is we cracked a coolant line in our tumble and now we may need a drag to the nearest service station."

"We can give you a lift," the hunter said. "We aren't barbarians, but," springs protested as he rubbed his fingers together, "nothing is free." A tall, muscular man with a green mohawk, and a short, lean woman with a shaved head and trench coat stood close guard. The woman shot Gracie a wink and a sly grin.

"One moment, I need to discuss this with my associates." Priest ducked back into the Queen Anne's Revenge, slamming the door behind him. They still had some meat and pelts left over from the swamp cats, but that wouldn't be enough. "Minister," he barked, "find me something we can offer to trade. We need to convince them to drag us on the final leg of this journey to the safety of a walled city." He scratched the stubble growing up his cheeks. "I would prefer to keep our ride for as long as possible."

"Sir," his minister said, "are you sure this is the best idea? We don't have a lot to trade and we still need to cross the river."

"I know that, you twit," Priest said, rubbing his temples. "But to cross the river, we need to get to the boatman, and to do that we need to get into the Crossing in the first place!"

"Couldn't we build a bridge," Gracie offered, "or ford across or something?"

"I like the way you think," Priest said, "but it's not an option." He sifted through a box of scrap and tools. "Plus there are more dangers, a thousand kilometers in both directions." He sighed, "believe me, I've given this extensive thought, and this is the only way we can do this. Voila!" He pulled a black box, covered in dials, gauges and buttons, from the back of a storage container. "If this doesn't convince our new friends to drive us into town, nothing will!"

They opened the Revenge to a firing range of gun barrels and crossbows cocked and ready to fire. "A fine distraction, indeed," the hunt leader said, smiling behind his mask. "We'll be happy to escort you to our city's finest holding cells, and kindly relieve you of your excess baggage!" He waved his gun in the direction of the stick shift. "Would you mind setting this thing into neutral, so we can tow it easier?"

Gracie stood, arms held above her head as their captors pawed through her pockets. A growing pile of guns, knives, grenades and a set of knuckle dusters collected around her feet. "You had all that, this whole time," Priest hissed. "You said you were low on ammo!"

Hunters outside the Revenge picked over dead boars, finishing the beasts off. The meat was toxic, but the bravest or stupidest butchers made the oily flesh their specialty. Gracie watched as the hunters butchered the herd and rooted through their sweetbreads. "What are they looking for," she asked.

"Specialized organs," Priest said. War boars feed on silicates, plastics, and metals. Their inorganic biology processes them. Nothing is too toxic or rough for their metabolisms." He grimaced. "They grow cybernetic parts. And their metallic tendons are still more efficient than spinning wires," he sniffed. "But we lost the art that bred their forebears centuries ago."

The hunters Priest came to think of as Baldy and Mo bound the three of them in heavy industrial tape. "Let's move," the hunt leader called out, bringing his people back to center. "Gather anything we can use. We're losing daylight, and we don't need another herd blindsiding us!" Someone shoved rough sacks reeking of old blood over their heads. "You," the hunt leader ordered Priest and his group, "get in with the guts and hold tight. We'll get you to town in one piece."

***

The truck carrying Priest and his party bounced over potholes and fallen debris. Burnt out vehicles piled in dead heaps on the side of the road, home to rats and snakes alike. Priest and Gracie did the best they could to keep from biting their own tongues off during the jostling. The minister had already swallowed his own tongue, a new one growing in its place. Twisted, gnarled trees grew upon grassy knolls laid out in strange grids.

"The scenery doesn't change much, does it," Priest said, attempting to break the awkward silence.

"They are going to find out who you are, and have us killed," Gracie said. "We are going to get killed and you are going to get shipped back to what's left of Kalkaska, for skinning and hanging." She stared at him through resigned eyes. She knew she was expendable, but didn't think she would be this expendable.

"They aren't going to kill him," Priest nodded to his minister. "If we're lucky, they might put us up for ransom. Your training and my knowledge make both of us too valuable, and as for him," the minister glared at him. "They would get frustrated soon enough. Haec fiunt."

"You are too optimistic about all this," Gracie said, gritting her teeth. "What happens when you are wrong about anything?"

"That's for us to find out. Until I'm wrong, I'm right, so we'll go with that for now."

"Damn it you are impossible," she said. The minister nodded, his tongue now at 50% but still not completely useful.

"Not impossible. It's my belief that I can manipulate random happenstance through the ether to at least come out in my favor."

"Optimist," she hissed again.

"Favorable realist," he declared.

"Shut up, both of you," the minister slurred around the stub of his tongue. He spat out a tarry wad of coagulated blood.

***

Like all city-states, Charon's Crossing's walls were monumental. The river was the city's defining feature, and like the continent as a whole, it split the city in two.

"Bienvenue á Charon's Crossing," the hunt leader announced. They had crossed the towering threshold. "The last armpit this side of the Acheron." Their eyes burned and they could feel the film of river air clinging to their skins. The sultry, humid southern climate sapped their strength.

"*Sanguis meus crassus est*," Priest moaned. "*Ego me explicare non possum*[12]."

Priest, Gracie and the minister eyed the heavy guns lining the city walls. "War boars and bandits. Both kinds of vermin need some big swatters," the minister said.

Gracie let out a low whistle. "I'm seeing shot cannons, EM coils and railguns," she said, "*abicite omnem spem, vos qui intratis*[13]." Even the guards bristled with augmented assault rifles, automatic shotguns and cattle prods.

"Lady and gentlemen," the hunt leader called out again, "if I may direct your attention to the northeast." In the distance a grim, dark tower stood out among lesser smokestacks, and water towers. "They call it the Devil's Stack, Lucy's Crack Pipe, Satan's Chimney," he rattled on like a bored tour guide. "She's over 800 meters high, used in part by the local foundries and smelters for exhaust from their ovens." He paused for effect. "Those ovens heat to over 5,000 degrees C. Much more than needed to melt tungsten. See," he said. "What they do in this city to criminals and traitors like yourselves isn't too pretty. They march them up to the lip of ol' Scratch's Pecker, crank the heat up, and you can calculate the rest." The hunt leader chuckled to himself.

"Alright," Priest shouted. The ambient city noise made him inaudible beyond a foot or two. "Considering this new tidbit of information, I have a plan." He licked his lips and blinked the sweat out of his eyes. "When we come to the next intersection, we'll all scramble out of this rig, barrel roll into the crowd. We'll blend in and regroup. Anybody have a problem with this?"

Gracie and the minister looked at Priest with tepid expressions and outright contempt. Finally, his minister sighed and lowered his head. "No," he said, at length. "I mean, if the

---

[12] My blood is thick/ I cannot explain myself.

[13] Abandon all hope, ye who enter here.

two of you get killed in all this, you're dead and that's that. I'll be stuck making my way one way or another," he spat, "forever," he said.

"I've heard worse plans," Gracie admitted.

"Good," Priest exclaimed, "It feels like we're starting to slow down now. Everybody ready!" To Gracie's surprise, Priest brought his hands from behind his back. He held some wire clenched in his fingertips. They went one by one. Priest led after picking their shackles. They tucked and rolled to freedom.

The hunters, their caravan and the Queen Anne's Revenge disappeared into traffic. The crowd and fog swallowed them within seconds. "How do we plan on getting her back, now that we're here," Priest's minister asked, a wry smile on his face.

"Good question," Priest said. "We need weapons and ammo, we need provisions and we need to cross that river." He proceeded to work on his minister's restraints. "The ferryman's price is steep but fair, but once he's paid, that is when the dangerous leg of our journey begins!"

"This sounds like one hell of a safari," Gracie grunted. "If you think what we've been through already was less than civilized, we should prepare for ten times worse. We'll need to hunt for every scrap of food, and don't get me started on guerilla warfare," she trailed off.

"Don't forget why we're going there," Priest snapped. "Once we find Eurydice alive," he gave it some thought and continued. "For the most part, at any rate, we can enjoy a restful smoke. Until then," he snapped his fingers and ventured into the crowd, sniffing the air, "I need sustenance. I have a powerful hunger for processed, reconstituted meat on a bun, and I don't think well on an empty stomach."

"How can you think of eating at a time like this," his minister hissed, looking for any sign of a tail. Gracie shared his paranoia, but her stomach was burning fumes as well, and the prospect of food was too good to deny.

"Simple," Priest said. If I don't find something that's already prepared, I'll have our bodyguard cut pieces from your shanks. Then, we'll have you roasted on a spit."

"Shut it with the cannibalism talk," Gracie barked. "Remember, it's my job to ride herd on you and keep you in line." She took a deep taste of the air, sniffing for the nearest food carts. The heady scents of grease and spice cut through the industrial odors. It cut the smell of burnt exhaust and molten metal.

"For which you are doing a smashing job," Priest said. "See if you can sniff us up a nice sit-down joint," he suggested.

"If we stop for food, we'll expose our position," his minister argued. "I mean, they had to have heard about Kalkaska and your betrayal by now."

"Shut it," Gracie snapped. "Cart food is fast and easy, and we can keep moving while we eat. We need to avoid errant eyes as much as possible," her head shot up and she sniffed, nose in the air, "Dogs! I smell dogs!" Gracie grabbed both men by their wrists. Then she dragged them into the seething crowds in search of grilled meat.

The food cart was a greasy mess, a dense swarm of grub bugs drinking up puddles of sauce and dog sweat. Bags containing fried snacks dangled from the awning. A cooler full of beer rattled on the concrete. The crowd surrounding the cart dispersed as Gracie stormed up to it, a fierce hunger in her eye.

"Sir," Priest said, shaking Gracie's iron grip away, "three of your finest meats on buns with the works." He winked. "Make them gross," he added. Thick, greasy steam rose from the heating racks, redolent of mystery meats. Gracie jabbed Priest in the ribs with her elbow and pointed to the bags lining the awnings. Priest sighed. "Throw in three packets of those crispy pig skins as well," he said. The minister jabbed him now and Priest continued, "three of your beers as well. Lagers if you've got them."

"Lookit chew, muthafukka," the vendor scoffed, kicking the cooler open. "We got beer," he continued, gesturing to an open cooler, clouds of condensation drifting out. A pyramid of white cans labeled BEER revealed themselves. Cylinders of mystery meat went on the bun, buried under a chunky wad of questionable chili. It could have been war boar chowder for all he knew. Synthetic onions and peppers crisscrossed the top in a crunchy lattice. "That'll be 25," the vendor said, not even looking at Priest and his compatriots.

"Twenty-five," Priest said, patting about his chest and hips, as if looking for his wallet. He looked at Gracie, "I seem to have left my billfold in the car, my dear. I don't suppose you could cover me this one time?" The grin on his face suggested that this would not be the last time, either.

Gracie stepped forward, wearing an aura of murder. Her account was always full, but this stretched their relationship. She was not a babysitter, not a nanny and not her ward's personal wallet. She handed over her card.

"I need 25," the vendor repeated, looking at her card with a frown. "What the hell is this? We deal in cash only, no trade or credit!" He snapped Gracie's card between his fingers and tossed them to the ground.

"There should be enough there," Gracie said. "I don't carry cash," she glared at Priest who whistled an innocent tune.

"I don't care if you have a million in that thing, I need 25 and I need it in my hand right now!" The vendor pulled a bat driven through with long nails from behind his cart. "We have ways of dealing with people who can't pay their way in this city. Police!" The vendor yelled at a pair of passing uniformed city defenders. "Oi, Reg! I've got some people here who seem to think these veg dogs grow on trees!"

Three giants in power armor clapped heavy metal hands on Gracie and Priest's shoulders. "Alright, people, you're coming with us," the guards said, grappling the trio into tight bear hugs. "We know what to do with travelers who think they can make their way through our walls on credit!"

"To hell with this," Gracie growled and rolled forward, throwing her guard into traffic. The minister followed her lead. He realized only too late that his arm reattachment was still fresh. The guard held on too tight, taking the minister's arm with him. Blood spewed from his shoulder into the officer's face plate. Without thinking, he snatched his arm back, swung it around and beat the guard with the wet end. It was only a brief moment, but enough of a surprise to relax his grip on Adeptus' shoulder.

"Run," he yelled at Priest, and brought his severed arm down on his own guard again. Gracie rolled under his feet and he tripped hard. "We'll get this figured out later!" Gracie rolled up to her feet and brought a boot heel down on the guard's throat. In another move, she reached over, driving her fist hard into the street vendor's face and grabbed his bat. It was now a common routine. She grabbed Priest and his minister, dragging them into the teeming masses. They disappeared as best as a wanted man, a bleeding amputee and their bodyguard could.

***

Can't
Race
Over
Silent roads
Suspicious movement
Takes our concentration away.
Hasty plans will be the deaths of us, I just know it.
Early dawn and I have their trail.
Arrived right on time.
Can't be late.
Hold back.
Eat.
Rest.
Other.
Now you change.
A small price to pay,
Sail away to the western shore.
Your destiny, like Eurydice, waits patiently.
Our meeting has yet to happen
Under desert sky.
Westward march.
Outlast
Us

I
Do not
Think that we
Have thought this plan out.
Eager hearts can make for rushed plans.
Resist the temptation to spring the trap this early.
Upset this critical balance
Blow him your kisses
If you lose
Chose now
One.
Now.
Put down
Our cards, dear.
If you think we'll win
Nobody likes a losing hand.
Take it or leave it, this is the point of no return.
Over the river, past the wastes
Face the western hills.
Never cross
Over!
Run
East!
Travel
Under moon
Race the coming day!
Never think I would lose my faith.

Chapter 9

"Looks like we're hidden for the moment," Priest said. "They've impounded our ride, and nobody is crossing the river until tomorrow." The ferryman kept quarters in a moldy shack adjacent the docks. The smell from the wharf alone was enough to strip paint. "What do we want to do until tomorrow?" AP Degory Priest, his bodyguard Gracie Caer and his minister hunkered down in the filth of an alley. They followed his shadow in the oily yellow light. The light came from a lantern hidden through faded curtains.

"We need to regroup and rest," Gracie said, checking the contents of her pockets. "This is a large enough city. We'll lay low and avoid the heat as best we can."

"We're keeping radio silence," the minister whispered. "But I've been seeing Kalkaska colors everywhere I look." He peeked around the corner of a rusty dumpster. As if to prove his point, a security agent wearing Kalkaska's colors strolled past.

"You worry too much," Priest hissed, "They've got bigger fish to fry now. They aren't going to waste time tracking us down." He sniffed. "Even if they did catch us, what are they going to do, bring us in and make us clean up our little mess? Skin us alive?" He shrugged, "Which do you think is more likely?"

"The skinning part," the minister said, rubbing his throat, "that takes weeks to heal."

"So, riddle me this, then," Priest said, dragging them out of the alley, "we are on the run, no vehicle, and no money. Where does one spend the night?"

"No-tell motel," Gracie suggested, "I'm sure there's a seedy brothel we can threaten with a good time." She shrugged and

83

pulled a few clips from around her person, "if we're lucky they'll accept bullets as currency."

"And what do we do with social misfits here," Priest jerked a thumb to his minister. "I like your thinking, but he may put our hosts… off." He looked his minister over and grimaced, "I mean, his face looks like a rotten Jack-O-Lantern," he said.

"Alright, I get it," the minister spat, "I'll stand guard in the muck and staph. I'm sure rats won't eat my legs by morning."

"That's the spirit," Priest chucked his chin. "We are all in agreement and can make sleeping arrangements. To the red-light district," Priest declared, rubbing his hands together. "We aren't shopping for treats," he said, reading his companions' expressions. "I'll set off a sanitation bomb, clear out the lice and funk," he pointed to Gracie. "You throw down some plastic tarps and we can start fresh in the morning." He held his hands out like a bad salesman making his worst pitch, "how does that sound?"

The minister spat a wad of phlegm and Gracie shuffled her feet. "What," he asked, "what's the problem with this plan?" He jabbed a finger at Gracie, "this was your suggestion, remember."

"No problem," she said, brushing her hair out of her face, "ideas and actions are all. I hope there's a private bathroom," she wrinkled her nose, "you guys are smelling worse than the river!"

The trio slipped through dark corridors and down busy streets, noses plugged. Priest stopped them for a moment. Pausing in a doorway, he removed a poke pocket inside his jacket and rolled three cigarettes. His lips curled up into a smile as Gracie doubled over, face beet-red and coughing.

"Sorry," he said, "I bred this for pipes; you're not supposed to pull it all the way in!" He waggled his eyebrows, tapped some ash and said, "Think of it more like a cigar!"

"God," Gracie gagged, eyes watering, "this smells worse than a dead war boar!"

"I needed something to cover the smell from the river," he said. "Let's try to find ourselves a decent pub," he continued.

They elbowed past a flamboyant pimp and what appeared to be a scantily-clad peacock. "I need to wash that protein dog down and I'm hoping the alcohol will help me forget the experience."

Neon and loud music pierced the gloom. They advertised everything from cheap booze to cheaper sex. Rich smoke and piano riffs fought frenetic techno and patchouli fumes. "I don't recall Kalkaska had anything resembling this," the minister breathed. Mesmerizing, heady aromas both exotic and noxious intoxicated them.

"They don't," Priest said, voice flat. "The good people of Kalkaska do their drinking like any good, god fearing people do: at home, in privacy. They have their own molecular reconstitution units. They wouldn't clutter up our fair city with all this." He waved a hand in the air, indicating the gaudy lights and transparent clothes.

"Looks like a fun time to me," Gracie said, eyeing the goods on display like a swamp cat drooling over a plump rat. A man in a harness winked at her and she licked her lips and winked back. "Bulla crustulum," she growled.

"It's undignified," Priest sniffed. "Here," he shoved past a pair of southerners failing to bribe their way into a locals only pub. "A normal dive with only booze on the menu. I need to think."

"Spoilsport," the minister said, scowling. "It's been your thinking that got us here, to this place, at this moment," he spat again. "Let's see where a little more thinking can get us."

"One more word out of you and I'll sell you on the cheap to a Tijuana war boar show," Priest snapped. He held the door open to a place marked Z for Gracie, but left it swinging for his minister. Smoke and incense poured out the door, smelling of a mixture of burnt food, and mutant blends of other things. "Barman," he roared into the darkened room, "prepare your alcohol, for I need to think!"

The bartender was a hulking thumb of muscle and chains. Bloodshot eyes glared from under thick, heavy brows at the travelers. "Ten seconds," he said through his teeth, "either order or get out! I'm done with undecided outsiders demanding attention!"

"Calm your tits, hothead," Priest soothed, "two beers and a broken jar of river water," he smiled. The bartender stood there, a thick vein in his forehead pulsing in time to the music on the jukebox.

"Two foamy browns and a sizzling moonshine," Gracie sighed, rolling her eyes, "they didn't let you out at all, did they?"

"One of fifty reasons I needed to get out of town." Priest took the two beers while Gracie grabbed a heavy mug full of viscous, muddy liquid. Her eyes watered from the fumes rising from the rim. They elbowed their way to one of the few available booths, tucked deep into the bar's darkest corner. Everyone was suspicious, but nobody paid them any mind.

"Now then," Priest said, dipping a chemical strip into his beer, "our plan."

"Yes," Gracie said, her lip mustached in foam, "the plan. What is it? It seems to change with the changing of the winds."

"Shut up, shut up," the minister hissed, "there are ears everywhere!"

"Nobody is listening," Priest said, twisting his earlobe, "I can't hear you over all the hubbub." A rich assortment of Charon's Crossing's worst elements packed the bar and the crowd got thicker by the minute. A thick cloud of smoke obscured the ceiling.

"Why plan at all if we get caught anyway," the minister asked, taking a nervous gulp from his drink. Sweat beaded on his forehead and fire ringed his eyes. He vomited bloody foam and fell convulsing to the floor. A few people looked with bemused interest at the new distraction but went back to their own business.

"Alright, if it means so much to you," Priest said, "we take the rest of today and a little tomorrow and regroup. We'll strengthen ourselves and collect our wits. Time is of the essence but if I know Eurydice, I know she can survive most anything for as long as she needs to.

"By tomorrow afternoon, we will make our way to the docks where we will negotiate our price with the ferryman. For most folks, it's a one-way trip so rates should be pretty reasonable."

"And then what," Gracie drank down the last of her beer in one final gulp. The local brew was stronger than the ales out east and she was having difficulty staying focused. "It's a long, dry walk to Orevada!" The minister twitched and gurgled a wordless confirmation from under the table.

"We need to find the Trinity Sisters," Priest said. "They don't encourage guests, but for anyone who can find them they do usually offer pretty good advice."

"They?" Gracie asked, her voice slurred. She was fighting a losing battle against double vision.

"The Trinity Sisters are that: sisters. Triplets. Identical triplets. They see things the way we do not; some say beyond our standard three dimensions."

"How do you know where to find them," the minister croaked, dragging himself back to his seat.

"I don't know how to find them," Priest said, "and nobody finds them- they find you. When they want to stay hidden, there isn't a tracker that could find them in the emptiest of the dry wastes." He let out a long, mellow belch and continued. "They do pal around with boar riders," he paused, scratching the scruff on his chin. "That could make them easier for us to find on our own, but then there's only one reason why anyone tames and rides war boars."

There was a loud crash and the crowd scattered to the outer perimeter. A pair of drifters in filthy road wear circled each other- long, ugly knives glittering in the dim light. In a flash they grappled, blades darting in and out to a chorus of shouts and screams. "Four to one on the long hair, seven to one on the denim jacket," the bartender shouted over the din.

"They're a lively bunch," Priest said, downing his beer. By the time he finished his glass, both men lay still. Blood mingled with peanut shells and cigarette butts. "It may be best we start heading for the door now," he said, eyes darting from one strange face to another. The wall of humanity thickened before the exit. "The longer we stay without ordering, the more likely someone is going to decide we don't belong here."

"My thoughts exactly," Gracie said. The minister looked down his nose at the mess.

"Pathetic," he sniffed as a barmaid dragged the corpses out the back. Nobody bothered to even mop up the twin trails of blood.

Charon's Crossing's red light district bred new families of sins few could imagine, much less please. The Neon God danced and cavorted from the tavern windows to brothel doors. Music and chatter poured from the doors of a thousand bars and brothels, but they didn't mask every sound. Behind every dumpster, freelancers did things even the most tolerant considered taboo.

"No vacancy," Priest intoned as they passed inn after hotel, "No vacancy, no vacancy, no vacancy." All three turned their heads as the bleating of livestock tumbled from a second story window. "At this point I'm willing to sleep on a park bench if need be."

A skeleton emerged from the shadows. Cheap mods took the place of her natural born eyes and her sockets were puffy with infection. "You need a place to sleep," she grinned with rotten teeth, "I know a place where you can lay down a bit." She gestured and vanished into the shadows.

"Here we go," Priest sighed, finally seeing a vacancy sign. "Odd Todd's meat pies, close shaves and rooms for the night, I don't see anything wrong with this, do you?"

Odd Todd's Inn was a dark, low, two-story structure with windows covered in aged newspaper and no music. Two men sat at the bar nursing drinks, and the bartender and his partner had gaunt, hungry looks on their faces. Priest gave them his brightest smile. "Two rooms and dinner for three, please," he placed his order with no introductions.

"We can give you one room if you're friendly enough," the bartender grunted. "The other room is in use," he said.

"Sounds cozy," Priest said, "we should only need it for tonight. Long travels ahead of us in the morning."

"We'll see," the bartender said, drawing four greasy mugs of skunky, off-brown beer. "City's been restricting who can go where." He licked his lips, "Where are you off to, then?"

"Western side of the river," Priest said, pulling a chair to a splintered table. "We're following people who," Gracie sat next to him and stomped on his foot. "Owe us money," he continued, wincing, "and we're quite motivated to get it back, aren't we fellows?" He elbowed his minister in the ribs.

"It's a pretty penny," the minister grunted. "Wouldn't be going if it weren't worth it."

"Better'd have cash to pay the boatman, then," the bartender said, slopping the mugs down. Foam oozed down the sides of the glass, "he's been raising his rates lately." His grin was humorless, "if you don't pay, he makes you swim."

"That sounds unpleasant," Gracie said, toying with her drink, but never actually drinking. With a practiced hand, she dipped a test strip into the liquid without anyone noticing.

"Usually it is," the bartender said, looking at her with his one good eye now. "How's the grub coming," he called back into the kitchen. Smoke billowed through the open window, belching the odor of pork in their direction

"Almost ready," a voice called back, "one of 'em tried to get away but I got the wily sumbitch!"

"Well hurry it up," he yelled back, "we've got customers consenting to eat!"

"We'll eat in our room, if that's alright," Priest said, smiling, "no rush."

"Suit yourself, cousin," the bartender said, "but so you know, there is no privacy here." A faded sign declared "Smile! You're on a hidden webcam!"

"Do anything too interesting there," he said, smirking at Gracie. "And you're going to have a big fan base, whether you want to be or not."

"Noted," Priest said, grabbing his key, "come along, compadres, we have travel plans to discuss!"

The room itself was as filthy as they expected it to be. Threadbare and bare bones, there was a stained, destroyed bed along one wall with a stained, torn up rug on the floor. The minister poked at a duffel bag hidden in the closet. It could have had a corpse or a love doll stashed inside but he wasn't that curious and its aroma gave no clues.

"Well," Gracie said, all five of her senses offended upon entering the room, "This is it. We are in hell."

"Nonsense," Priest said. "It needs a little cleaning, some TLC, a tasteful floral print and all this could be as charming as home!"

"It needs a can of kerosene and a match," the minister said, closing the closet door. "I've crawled through sewers with better sanitary conditions."

Gracie nodded, jaw set. "I'm almost tempted to take my chances in the alleyway."

"Look, if we lay our coats down on the bed, we may only get a few social diseases and a handful of parasites by morning." He gave the mattress a dubious look.

"Alright," Gracie sighed, "I'm sure food will be along shortly. What's our brilliant plan to cross the river and meet these fortune tellers of yours?" She swatted a cockroach from the sagging dresser and sat on it instead of any other surface in the room. "You said these sisters might have a lead on our quest?"

A smile spread across Priest's lips. "I am so glad you asked," he said.

Chapter 10

Leaving their motel had been a discreet but unnerving game of nap-and-dash. "We need to cross this river yesterday," Priest whispered. They squeezed shoulder to shoulder down littered back alleys. "Our welcome has worn itself out."

"I'll take the lead," Gracie said. Her nose guided them down the polluted artery piercing the city's black heart. "You," she said to the minister, pressing a small handgun into his hands, "make sure we don't grow a tail."

"Loud and clear," he said, feeling the weapon's weight in his hand before checking the chamber. Priest often issued similar ghost guns when it was his day to clear the mutants from the service shafts. They often lacked charge or ammo. Priest's sense of humor was infamous.

The river's stench strengthened with every footstep. Priest followed a worn map he dug from the furthest reaches of his pack. Despite his assurances, they found three unique paths to the same brothel as the day dragged on. "We've passed this same Bunny Club four times now," Gracie pointed out. The minister smirked. Priest's face blazed a shade reserved for third-degree sunburns and stop signs. He cursed, balling the map and did his best to punt it into the nearest garbage can, missing by yards.

They rounded another corner, and came face-to-face with a mob. A sea of faces stared them down without a hint of emotion. "Um," Gracie bit her lip. A thousand eyes sang her a ballad of torture and betrayal. A thousand bulletins bearing their faces was all she needed to back up that desperate tale.

Priest looked from one face to another. The air hung heavy with the odors of smoke, spice and sex. If breathing were drinking, this neighborhood was a thick milkshake with extra bobas. "I am going to do something," he whispered, "and when I do, you duck, roll and run, understand?"

"Duck?" Gracie hissed, eyes darting from one grubby face to the next, "Run where?"

"NOW!" The second Gracie saw the Bouncing Betty, she grabbed the minister's shoulders. Then, she shoved him to the ground. The pavement was sticky under her bare arms. Priest dropped, covering his ears as he threw the world's worst party gag to the ground. It spun like a top throwing shrapnel everywhere at chest height.

Barbed spikes found themselves buried up to three inches in nearby brick walls. Priest leapt his feet, dragging Gracie and his minister along. It was everything they could do to keep their balance in the midst of such carnage. They passed a gun back and forth, picking assailants off in their wake. Gracie dropped a few smoke grenades and pulled the two men into a shady alcove away from prying eyes.

All roads funneled them towards the docks. "Here we go," Priest said, relieved and triumphant. "Everyone check your pockets because this won't be cheap!" Even now through the smoke, they could see the shadows of the locals searching for blood. Priest and his party doubled their pace, pitching headlong towards the wharf.

"Hey," Priest hailed the boatman. A face with skin turned to leather from a lifetime of cheap tobacco and grain alcohol turned to greet them. He smiled, revealing he had more fingers than teeth. Priest tore open his jumpsuit, exposing two chips of shiny metal taped to his chest. "I will pay for this last second ride, but we need to be on that western shore yesterday, you understand?"

***

Most people knew the river used to have bridges. But, they also knew the last one went down long ago before their great-great-grandma was out of trainers. Back then, boatmen used steam engines, oars, and poles to ferry people from one side to the other. When things were good, everyone had food on the table. But then the war boar population skyrocketed and the Wild Hunt came through, destroying farms and cities alike. Travelers became scarce and boatmen vanished. We all heard about the ones who got taken by the Hunt or eaten by boars, or those who lost fights with rival boatmen.

As time went on, the world got darker. The boatmen disappeared one by one, until only one remained - the boatman at Charon's Crossing.

***

The boatman looked from the coins, to the thick smoke and crowds of confused, angry vigilantes. "Sounds good to me," he said with an easy smile, "seems to me like you are in a little hurry?" With a couple tugs of a cord, the ferry roared to life with loud reports and bursts of blue smoke. "Let's see if we can work something out."

The old man's rusty boat held together with layers of patches. Priest, Gracie, and his minister bundled in as they could, trying to not rock the boat. They bobbed a little, but the boatman didn't immediately pull away from the docks.

"Well," Priest said, slapping the side of the gondola, "are we going or are we staying to enjoy the scenery?"

"Nope," the boatman said with a drawl, "ain't nothing pleasant about this river, that's for sure." He pulled a greasy hand rolled cigarette from his shirt pocket and lit it. "If anything, I need some assurance you'll pay before we cross to the other side."

"Assurance?" Priest seethed. "Good god, man, if you don't get us going they'll drag us all back and they'll skin you alive before you even see a penny!"

"See, that strikes me as motivation," the boatman said, gesturing with the cherry end of his smoke. "Motivation for negotiation." He cackled at his turn of phrase.

"Fine, fine," Priest said, peeling a coin from his skin, wincing as his chest hair came out, "take the damn money."

"Wise man," the boatman said, catching the coin in midair, "you're smarter than you look!" He flicked ash from his cigarette into the feted waters and a spark of flame lanced the air where it landed.

The sticky river water flowed with a current, smelling like alcohol or trichloroethylene. Spotlights on both sides of the river illuminated the boatman's way, fumes dancing in the beams. The opaque water hid something fleshy and powerful, working against the current.

"I know what you're thinking," the boatman said. Priest watched the ropy appendages drifting around. "Lamprey-squid had a hatch the other week. You wouldn't make it five yards before they snagged you." He chuckled again.

"Now this one," he said, indicating the minister, "he's got some piss 'n' vinegar in him." He puffed on his cigarette. "Lamprey-squid can be mean, especially during mating season." He gave a knowing wink to the minister.

"Mating season?" Gracie's stomach did a flip and she felt her gorge rise. War boars, cannibals and mutants were nothing compared to randy parasitic cephalopods.

"See, they aren't all that bright," the boatman explained. "Being naught but tentacles and sucker-mouths. When it comes to mating season, they get to thinking about anything in the water as a potential partner." He shuddered. "I've seen things a month spent in an opium den couldn't erase."

Smoke cleared by the time they reached the middle of the river, an outraged crowd gathered on the shore. Those with sense had gone home. Those who felt the need to prove something kept pace with Priest's boat. Rocks, bottles and a few shoes fell short of the boat, stirring up the ferocious squid.

Priest could not resist and lifted both middle fingers into the air for all to see. The crowd's anger peaked and they jostled harder onto the rotten docks. Eldritch wood groaned and bent under their weight, but still they ignored the danger. Gracie and Priest watched with mixed emotions as the planks gave way. Dozens of rioters plunged into the water. Some came back up, their flesh pink and raw with chemical burns as they struggled to evacuate the river.

Lamprey-squid that had once circled the little boat immediately set upon the swimmers. Gracie tried to block the screams out, but the water churned frothy and pink as the beasts set upon their prey. Priest sat mesmerized as hooked tentacles pulling dozens of people under the surface. The minister bummed a smoke from the boatman.

The screams faded as the boat reached the western shore. "Jesus," Priest whispered, breathing hard. He stole his minister's cigarette and took a deep drag.

"I told you, you shouldn't watch," the boatman said, monitoring his boat through the viscous liquid. "First time I saw a feeding frenzy like that," he paused as though he were recalling yesterday's lunch. "These docks were a lot busier, a lot more boats going from the east to the west. Big collision between two ferries sent hundreds down to a fate I wouldn't wish on the war boar that ate my own mother!"

His cigarette had gone out and he lit it with an ancient, oily lighter. "Not too much farther now," the boatman said, squinting through the gloom. All was quiet on the western shore.

"Any news from beyond the Plains," Priest asked, "any rumors of the Walking Sisters?"

"Not too much," the boatman said. "Most of what we hear doesn't come from more than 20 clicks beyond the river." He spat. "What do you want to know about the Sisters anyway," he asked. "When you get past the lies and the stories, they ain't nothing but trouble."

"Never mind," Priest grumbled, "anyone recently tried to head east? Any travelers from Orevada?"

"Nope," the boatman said. He adjusted his motor as the water grew more viscous. "Other than the locals we don't get much west-east travel for a couple of months now." He smiled, "you're my first fare in a couple of weeks now, come to think of it."

Something large and terrible caressed the boat's hull with a groan. "You may see a few tribes of boar riders, but they tend to keep to themselves. Bandits are more likely to tear you apart before you come across them, or they you."

The boatman took a long, final drag on his cigarette and threw the butt into the thick water. A pink-gray tentacle covered with questing suckers grabbed it. "Orevada is gone. I've heard some rumors of a warlord emerging from the desert or the mountains, depending on whom you talk to. They even say he commands the Wild Hunt like his own army but that's boar-shit," he laughed.

"Now," the boatman said, bringing the boat to a stop short of the docks, "we need to complete the payment." He pulled out another cigarette and lit it with a snap of his lighter.

"Do you take an IOU," Priest asked. "I'm sure we will need the other coin for," he waved his hand, "I don't know, supplies, or a sandwich."

The boatman shifted the joint from one corner of his mouth to the other and sniffed. "You can pay me what you owe me," he said with ice in his words, "or you can swim." The water boiled with lamprey-squid and caustic fluids sizzled on their mucous flesh. "Hope you are good swimmers," he said.

Gracie's hand drifted to the knife on her belt, but the boatman saw her game. "Go ahead," he said, "see what happens when you stick that in me and you can't figure out how to work the motor." He laughed with no joy. "The river is so strong it'll carry you down stream 100 kilometers, but the hull will dissolve before you make it even 75." He spat thick phlegm into the river. "Tick-tock," he said, "make your decision: pay me, stick me or go swimming; I don't have all day but I know I can be a lot more patient."

Priest pondered for a moment. "Fine," he said, "we don't have enough time for negotiations. Gracie, you have my permission to open him up." Gracie smiled and drew out seven inches of razor sharp steel.

The boatman's eyes opened wide at the sight of the blade, but decades of experience made him strong and balanced. He bared his yellow teeth and growled; with a single motion, he kicked an oar into his hands, raising it. "Go ahead," he hissed, "you ain't got the stones and I've sent better than you into the soup!"

"Wrong," she said, still smiling. Holding his attention on her knife, she dropped a long, tapered dart from her sleeve to her free hand. With a flick of her wrist, the blackened steel spine found its home in the boatman's eye socket. He didn't even cry out as his knees buckled and he fell hard into the water.

"Alright, time for a course in quick-study," Priest said. He gloated over the ancient, crusty motor. Priest had watched the boatman start the motor and pulled the frayed ripcord. He sniffed in disappointment. "Here he had me up for a challenge," he said. "Minister! Jerk!" It took the minister a few attempts, but it sprang to life with a few violent reports and a burst of blue smoke. A rooster tail of thick water flew up and the boat swayed, until Gracie and Priest balanced the boat. The current had taken them downstream a few kilometers but not far.

"Let's go upriver," Priest said. "If the boatman is a no-show, they'll be on us like dry blood on a war boar."

As if in response, searchlights flared on, stabbing bright circles onto the water. Gracie and the minister both rolled their eyes. "God damn but your timing is impeccable," she said.

Priest rubbed his eyes. "Minister," he said, "do your best to keep us out of the lights. We may have a bit of a boat ride ahead of us."

if the minister sighed, it went unheard. The little boat was maneuverable even as they fought the current and debris. The boatman's body had disappeared below choppy waves. Shadows were already waving from the western shore.

"I'll take us as far as the fuel lasts," the minister said, tapping the gauge. The needle rattled but seemed to stay at about a third of a tank. "Once we hit the final quarter, it doesn't matter where we are." He scratched his nose. ``Either we land, or we drift our way back down past the Styx to the Sinus Dolorum.''

They rumbled north, leaving no wake, leaving the shouting and searchlights behind. Tree-crowned cliffs loomed on either side above the drowned skeletons of river boats. Campfires marked hidden travelers among the trees on long, narrow islands. The islands were far enough away to guarantee privacy and discourage socializing. Priest liked this best.

They made their way to the western shore, without incident. They slipped between the pylons of fallen bridges, careful not to make waves. No eyes marked their passage.

Chapter 11

A long time ago, an Adeptus Physicus, his minister, and their guard hid under a counter in a ruined diner. Broken roads and walls separated them from the wasteland. Scavengers picked at dead bodies on the ground. The clouds and the surroundings made it hard to hear.

They had taken to hiding when it became clear they were being tracked. Backs pressed to a broken, burnt wall, they waited for the most opportune time to run.

"Do you see anything," Priest whispered to Gracie, who was angling a tiny mirror on a stick over the counter.

"Not since the last three times you asked," she hissed, "now be quiet!"

"What if we could outrun it," the minister suggested, "or leave some bait as a distraction?"

"No such luck," Gracie whispered, "we've all heard it snuffling about; it's going to want more than a strip or two of jerky." Her stomach growled and she punched it. "You're more than welcome to try your little experiment with your ration." She scanned with her mirror some more. "And further, we don't want to ring the dinner bell for any of its friends!" She lowered her mirror and took a sip from her canteen. Water was low and she couldn't remember the last time she had a smoke or a bath. She could feel her baser nature getting antsy.

She needed to power through the next three days, she needed to stay sharp. Every second Gracie was above the grass was a good second, and she aimed to keep those seconds coming.

"What if we threw up a thermo sphere," the Minister suggested. "Get a lock on the heat signature of every moving entity in a 10-mile radius and we can get the drop on it."

"Right," Priest said, rolling his eyes. "Let's throw a big ol' glowing ball up in the air and mark our position! Let's go ahead and do that!" Gracie poked her mirror around the corner. The questing snuffles and snorts sounded like they were edging farther away. Holding a finger to her lips, she did her best to sign that the coast seemed clear. The next stack of ruins was a quick dash away.

Adjusting her gun for incendiary rounds, Gracie signaled the two men to run. How they managed to survive was beyond her. Staying low and running light, she caught up with the two scientists, dragging them into the dirt. She clamped hands clamped over their mouths. The wall they now hid behind was even lower and crumbling, but it was opaque.

"I'm curious," the minister whispered once her damp fingers left his lips, "isn't there another route? Couldn't we be a little more direct? It feels like we've been going in circles."

"Yes," Gracie hissed. "And they will have those routes watched." She risked a peek through a window, finger on her trigger. "I mean, if we're lucky it might be bandits who would only murder and rob us. Or at least murder us," she shuddered. "Right now we have more immediate concerns."

None of them had seen the beast in the brambles but everything they'd observed was too unsettling. Even more unsettling, there was no way to tell how many things were stalking them. Gracie sniffed the air, but everything smelled bad. The odor was nothing compared to the river, but she still wrinkled her nose at it. Gracie could detect the distinct bouquet of moldy bike shorts and burning tires.

"Come on," she whispered, motioning them to run to the next mound of rocks and rubble. They rounded a corner and immediately heard footsteps. Gracie cocked her gun and looked back and forth for anything moving. A bag rustled and she unleashed hell. Burning phosphorus and lead sprayed in all directions until everything resembled burnt meat.

Gracie's chest heaved, sweat pouring down her face as her gun clicked over the empty chambers. Priest pushed the barrel of her gun down, his hand shaking. "Nice shooting, sheriff," he cracked.

There were no sounds, but if nothing knew about them before, they did by now. She popped her spent ammo drum and slammed a fresh magazine home. "Be ready for anything," she whispered.

Gracie's world spun. They stood in a circle, Gracie and the minister guns out while Priest pulled the pin on another grenade.

A war boar, all alone, rounded the corner and faced them. Its eyes glowed with madness while thick fluids dripped from its snout. It was on its last legs, dead flesh and organs clinging to its cybernetic frame. "Nobody moves," Priest cautioned. "Nobody makes any sudden movements. It's weak and disoriented, and they're unpredictable when they're like this."

The creature's skin clung to its bones like a well-worn bathrobe. A single eye flickered with madness in a fractured socket. Once a war boar's organic metabolism died, they switched to auxiliary power. Pulsing, grinding, unlubricated machinery lurched under broken ribs. Its broken lower jaw hung open, blood and oil caking its face and matting its spiky hair.

Priest circled around it, not once taking his eyes from the monstrosity. The stench of rotting tissue and oxidation belched from tattered, wheezing lungs. "Shoot it," he pressured Gracie. "Shoot it dead, shoot it in the head, shoot it, shoot it, shoot it!" He was around another wall and wheezing. Its hunger was an illusion spun from computer memory rather than any need for nutrition.

The minister snuck past, eyes locked on the hell-pig. Dead muscles lined with fine steel cable tendons flexed with purpose as it grunted. Blood, drool and motor oil dripped and pooled from its ragged muzzle. It was like staring down a rabid bulldozer.

Gracie and the war boar circled each other like a pair of gladiators, guns and tusks ready to kill in a split second. The pig moved in a long, slow circle, fluids dripping and entrails dragging. Gracie turned with it, gun level, finger on the trigger, prepared to unleash flaming hell upon its face.

Time froze and the war boar shrieked with a roar of grinding servos, bolting full speed at Gracie. She screamed her battle cry, pumping round after round of burning flechettes, as fast as she could. It was all she could do to keep up with the beast as it ducked, dodged and wove around her assault. It closed the gap between itself and its small, fleshy dinner.

Sweat gushed down Gracie's face as a cave of black, rusty tusks gaped over her like a tsunami. Hot, stinking breath forced its way into her sinuses.

With a twist of its head, it knocked the wind out of her chest and sent her flying into a wall slab 10 feet behind her. She dropped her gun and fell to her knees. She bowed to the gaping hole of jagged teeth and tusks. She didn't know if war boars could gloat, but she could feel its malicious satisfaction before her. Then it would go after the others.

Gracie closed her eyes tight, teeth clenched and anticipating the killing bite. The moment came and went, her chest heaving in panicked contractions but the bite didn't come. She opened one eye, and then the other, not sure if she was ready to see what lay on the other side. The war boar was dead with two long chunks of steel rebar impaling it. Two long wires led from the rebar to a massive ancient but functional battery.

"Thank you," she panted, picking herself up. "Thanks for that." There wasn't an inch of her body that wasn't trembling or soaked in sweat.

"Lucky find, eh," Priest helped her up while the minister rooted around in the monster's body cavity. "Everyone should be alert. I have a feeling there may be more like this one lurking about." Everything the minister collected went into a small bag he strapped around his chest. "We can get some good trade off those components," Priest said. "Let's step lively though. We've wasted enough time as it is."

"Why haven't they hunted those things to extinction," Gracie asked. She assisted Priest over the remains of a fence on their circuitous journey. "That thing wasn't alive, but it sure as hell wasn't dead either!"

"They exist because they can," Priest said with no expression. "Their purpose was to clear battlefields of the dead and wounded, and they were very good at it."

"Why not nuke the battlefield," Gracie asked, "or set funeral pyres?"

"For the kill, yes," Priest said, "but then what about after? You can't use land saturated in radiation."

"I suppose," she said, looking around a tight corner and breathing a sigh of relief.

"And human cleanup crews are expensive," he counted on his fingers. Robots malfunction. Necro-parasites are a fun prank on research assistants, but they usually backfire."

"How much further before we are out of here," Priest's minister asked. "It feels like somebody's watching us."

"Well, someone is," Priest said, "here," and with a swift motion he brought his heel down hard on the war boar's glass eye.

The ghost town labyrinth thinned the farther they walked. To Gracie and the minister's mutual delight, there were no further sightings of war boars. They could hear several of them lost in the wastes and saw markers of their passing, but stayed out of their way.

"So, what are we looking for, once we get out of here," the minister asked. "You said you wanted to track the Walking Sisters. How do you plan to do that?"

"I've heard stories," Priest said, "There is a wandering caravan led by three sisters. No one sees them unless they desire it, but aren't above a little compensated persuasion." He reached into the minister's pack for one of the artificial organs. "If you bring the heart of a war boar, and if you think real loud that you have one, they might decide to reveal themselves."

"And why do you want to meet with the sisters," Gracie asked. "They know something you don't?"

"Let's say they can see things better than most people," Priest said. "A lot of the time their advice can be a touch cryptic." He shrugged. "But that's how it goes with these kinds of things."

The light was fading into evening as they reached the farther end of the suburban wasteland. "We need to find some shelter," Gracie said, "with war boar about, we need to be scarce, pronto."

"Check for alcoves, basements or bomb shelters," Priest said. "Anywhere there might be a cache or reserves." This time it was his stomach's turn to grumble with rage. "We've been living off the land too long."

Shadows stretched out long, malevolent fingers attracting large, black birds from their nests. Daytime sounds transitioned to evening sounds. Insects buzzed and thrummed while herds of unseen animals ceased their snuffling.

The sun was almost gone by the time they found the heavy steel blast doors. "Success," Priest cheered, "we can at least get some sleep!" Ancient, rusty chains held the doors shut, a cryptic message painted across it. Gracie pulled out her hunting knife and did the honors, breaking the chain with a twist of her wrist.

Beyond the doors and spread below them lay a chamber of horrors. The room had been an emergency shelter, but it proved to be the occupants' undoing. Stiff, desiccated remains of dozens of poor souls revealed a long-forgotten massacre. Those closest to the doors crushed to death under so many others trying to escape. Corpses deeper in telling a tale of aggressive cannibalism. Everywhere limbs lay strewn and broken, tooth marks still pressed deep into bone. The minister looked on at the charnel house, but Gracie and Degory struggled not to gag.

"Those poor sons of whores," the minister breathed. "What do you suppose had gotten into them?"

"If I had my guess," Priest said, casting a beam of light into the room, "we may have stumbled on one of those practical jokes."

Gracie squinted at the faded paint on the blast doors. "Don't open," she read, "dead inside. I thought you said reanimating the dead was something done to the other guys?"

"These might have been those other guys," Priest said, a bitter smile on his lips. "One thing is for sure, though," he said, snapping his light off and standing up, "we have a decision to make."

"A decision," Gracie Caer said, brow furrowed, "what decision? Do we find another hole in the ground or do we find a level space to pitch a tent?"

"Oh we're staying right here," Priest said. "Safety demands it. What we need to decide is, do you want the top or bottom bunk?"

Gracie stared at him. "What," she demanded, "the hell is wrong with you?"

"Everything," Priest said, "I am alive and wish to continue to remain so. Once my little quest is complete, you are free to go on your merry little way," he said, smiling.

Gracie and the minister sorted through the pit. Everywhere, dry, bony hands reached the door for unattainable salvation. Birds circled overhead, crying to each other, calling dibs on the three below.

"Clear them out," she said, finally. "Clear them all out. But make sure this place airs out well," she shook her head. "And burn them once they're all out." She spat on to the ground, hoping she wasn't breathing mold spores. "Burn them all."

Priest grinned. "I thought you might see it my way. S'mores are on me tonight," he said. He was far too cheerful.

Chapter 12

The sun beat down on Adeptus Degory Priest, his minister, and his bodyguard Gracie Caer. They did not speak, their jaws aching as they clenched and ground their teeth to stubs. The western shore, their initial goal, offered little for food, water or hope.

Big, black birds made lazy circles overhead against the bright disk of the sun.

"I'm hot," Priest broke the silence, "tell me again there is a town or something coming up."

"We're all hot," Gracie snapped, "stop bellyaching. And for the last time, if there is a settlement I'm sure it's swarming with bandits or ghouls." She paused and gave it a thought. "If we're unlucky they might even be bandit-ghouls or ghoul-bandits, perish the thought."

"Not exactly my problem," the minister said. "I'm looking for some shade." Any trees still standing were small, dry and skeletal, exuding a foul, oily corrosive sap. The black birds perched in these trees and encouraged the trio to give into their suffering.

"Shade is for those who've earned it," Gracie growled, "now trudge in silence, your voice is driving me to a stroke."

"We should all be silent," the minister hissed. "We don't have enough water to support your griping."

More black birds joined the flock between one hill and the next.

"Will we at least be meeting the Weird Women soon," the minister asked, dehydration the last thing on his mind. "I'm saying, the life of a pack mule is a difficult one." He shifted his bag in a vain attempt to redistribute the weight across his shoulders.

"One more word and I'll dismember you," Priest warned. "And you don't plan on meeting the Weird Women, they plan on meeting you." He took a deep breath of hot air and regretted it. "When they want to stay hidden, they're impossible to find. If they know you have positive intentions and something to trade, they'll turn up. The key is to stay mobile and optimistic."

"That's too many maybes for my liking," Gracie said, sweat staining her back and armpits. "I don't suppose we could speed things up with a signal flare or two?"

"Efficient," Priest snorted. "If you want to ring the dinner bell for every bandit, mutant and war boar on this side of the river. But please, be my guest. Do me a favor and let me get a running head start!"

"I don't like it," Gracie said, eyeing their surroundings. "We'll be fine if it's a small group, but if we're facing a raiding party, we may be up Two Deuces Creek."

"You worry too much," Priest said. "And besides, if anyone was going to turn our bones into fashion accessories, I'm sure it would have happened by now."

"If this keeps up, I may turn your scrote into a change purse before I feed you to an ant hill," Gracie grumbled.

"I'll hold him down," the minister chimed in.

"Enough of the sour words and crumpled faces," Priest said with a smile. "Why, from these very hilltops you can still see the stagnant fumes rising from the river!" A bird cackled in the distance. He bit his lip, "I suppose we'll find some friendly travelers. With any luck they may be willing to barter goods or services." He rattled his canteen. "Or food or water."

"Bite your tongue," Gracie snarled. "Out here I wouldn't take the time of day if they offered."

"Hope you enjoy walking," Priest said. "I'm serious, the loss of the tank was a low blow. We've lost too much time." They trudged on in wrathful silence as the birds continued their slow wheel against the sun.

Thunder and lightning shattered the sky bringing a squall of heavy rain and hail. All three stopped dead, steam rising from their shoulders in the fragrant humidity. Priest sighed. "Keep walking, everyone," he said. "We're more likely to find shelter if we keep moving."

"Not holding my breath," Gracie grumbled.

"I can't imagine anything being dry after this," the minister grumped.

"Now, come on," Priest said as they plodded on, every raindrop a slap to the face. "A little walk in the rain will build some character!"

"Tell us, Priest," Gracie shouted over the thundering rain, "how did you come to meet your sweetie? Give us the juicy details!" His minister retched in mock nausea.

"It's complicated," Priest said. "Things were a whole lot different then."

"Such specificity," Gracie said, rolling her eyes.

"The Order of the Adeptus Mechanicus used to have more control," Priest said. "We felt like kings, and basically, we were! We were on fire, always making exciting discoveries. We blazed new trails into the future to help humanity and a few other species too." Taking a break, he wiped rain from his eyes. "I was a simple physicist who dabbled in genetic engineering. She worked on bionics and fancy surgeries," he added, lost in thought. "Together, we made new, exotic energy sources. We tried teleportation and bioengineering."

He smiled, continuing, "the arts and techniques we crafted would have had us burnt as witches long ago. It was by our combined efforts we held the darkness of the Wild Hunt at bay." This time it was the minister's turn to roll his eyes, making his hand squawk like a verbose duck.

"Then came the wars," Priest persisted. "And they corrupted our research and technology. Tin-pot dictators made us executioners instead of teachers and priests. All they wanted was a better bomb or gun!" He thrust his fist into his palm. "False Imperators and war-chiefs did nothing but lay waste to the world around them. They blighted the land and poisoned the water! They branded us Conpedibus hominibus, the Shackles of Man." Priest spat the bitter words from clenched teeth.

"The wars waned and power shifted with the wind, as it always does," he said, "the time of the kings, gods and emperors ended. The people rose up and smashed the old symbols bringing forth a new world of their own design. They understood they couldn't destroy us. The sum of our knowledge was too vital and valuable to lose forever, but they could separate us." Rainwater built up into growing rivulets around their ankles as they walked. "We made a pact. We would be together again, come hell or high water, or high water in hell. Nothing matters more than that to me at this point. I will feed a herd of chinchillas to a war boar if it means our reunion."

A visceral scene of advanced modern art spread out before them as they crested another hill. A feeding frenzy of war boars writhed and shrieked in a small lake of mud and blood. Black, greasy birds, attracted to the sound and smell circled high above. Priest and his team leapt into the mud behind a fallen log. They had gone unnoticed despite the beasts' horrifying sensitive senses.

Gracie drew her long gun, gazing at the scene through her night vision scope. "If I time it right, I can take 80 percent of them out with a single mag," she said, squinting through her scope.

"And while you're reloading," the minister said, "the remaining 20 will be turning the rest of us into pig shit."

"Have some faith in our guardian," Priest whispered. "If you swallow a couple of those grenades before you get eaten you would be the perfect Trojan Horse."

"Getting devoured before exploding. What more could a boy ask for," the minister growled.

"It would be your last great act of defiance," Priest said. "You know, before you got yourself back together."

"You turned me into a protein shake and drank me. I still have nightmares of the contents of your septic tank."

"Well if we can't kill them we'll need to sneak around them," Gracie said, "do you have any suggestions?"

"Roll around in the mud," the minister whispered. "War boars' sense of smell is twice as good as their hearing." He shrugged. "But that's only taking two of their 10 senses into account."

"I'm leaning toward using you as a distraction," Gracie responded. "Priest and I can get past and you catch up when you're able." Priest nodded in fervent agreement.

"We can save the innuendo for later," Priest whispered. "Give the swine a few minutes, their numbers should be more in our favor and we can make our final decision then."

The sea of sharp bristles and noisy pigs cleared leaving a blood-stained crater. Pieces of flesh and biosteel scattered across the slick grass. The remaining pigs, injured and feeble, their engines roaring with intense hunger. Using a field glass, Priest evaluated their current circumstances. "I can salvage some parts there. But, you need to kill the remaining survivors," he said. "Act swiftly. Our objective isn't to extend dinner invitations any further."

"Got it," Gracie said, her trigger finger itching. With a few quick bursts of fire, the quarreling boars sprawled out to join their dead peers. "Done and done," she said, slinging her gun to her back. "Say the word next time you need something shot."

"I will keep you posted," Priest said, giving his minister a side eye. "I may allow you to use this one as target practice." The minister sighed as he picked himself up.

Priest and his minister dug through viscera while Gracie monitored the horizon. It seemed like they couldn't stop anywhere for long before the next shoe dropped. There wasn't a dive bar or roach motel for miles where he could be safe from trackers and bounty hunters.

For how exposed Priest felt on the western shores of the Acheron, he was still glad to be there and in one piece. For how bad those beasts stank, nothing could compare to the unwholesome stench of that river. And for how horrifying the boars had been, they still didn't compare to the mutated life that dwelt in the water.

Chapter 13

The night time passed while the sleepers rested tight in sanctuary. The morning sun rose, waking a mad cockatrice whose shrieks broke the dawn. Gracie rousted the Adeptus and his Minister. "Time to get going," she said. Fragrant smoke rose from the glowing ember in her clay pipe.

A stack of ashes lay beyond the sepulcher, smoldering in the morning sun. Priest's minister, with Gracie the Praetorian, spent hours making sure nothing remained. Aromatic smoke rose in a tower, marking their passage. The long, overgrown highway lay at their feet. Gracie split rations, weapons and polished synthetic organs into their bags.

Priest slung his bag now laden with cans of food over his shoulder. Someone left a cache hoping their refuge would last but they had no chance. "Their misfortune is our benefit," he smiled, looking at the sealed tin, its label long since faded. "If any of this is still good, we will eat like kings at our next camp!"

"What was that place," Gracie asked after some time. "There were doors leading deeper into the facility past our camp." She reflected on the bones covered in bite marks and those splintered apart for the marrow. "That wasn't any basement. Someone sealed and barricaded those doors from the inside. What was that place?"

"They sealed it from the inside for a reason," Priest said. "We weren't meant to go any deeper," he continued. "I found documents that suggested that the place was a research facility." He wiped his face. "Focus was on the military applications of biotechnology." He tutted. "They were digging into forces they weren't prepared to control. How ironic."

They walked half a day before hunger forced them to break. Priest piled wood into a small stone circle, nodding to Gracie to give it a burst from her flamethrower. Priest picked through the food, his stomach making many threats it intended to keep. He could feel Gracie and his minister's famished eyes boring holes into his back. "Spoiled," he judged one can, throwing it into a bush. "I judge rotten," he concluded with another. There were many cans, but only now could he see their use by dates had passed. He rummaged some more, finally finding a few cans of good food they could eat.

"Oranges," Gracie read out loud, squinting at the faded labels. "This one says onions and the third says," she made a face, "tinned sardines. You two can eat stew, I'm going hunting." She slapped a clip into her gun and adjusted for small game. With luck there would be something small, furry and full of meat scampering about.

Gracie did not even make it 20 yards before Priest called her back. "What," she demanded, "do you want?" Hunger and rage danced in her black eyes.

"I don't think we have," he said, "a can opener. Do you?"

Gracie closed her eyes and took a deep breath. Faster than a snake, her hunting knife found its mark between Priest's knees as he sat on his log by the fire. "For the record," she said, giving him a side-eye, "I was considering aiming for your scrote." She sniffed and set off down the game trail.

Game was hard to come by. There was some small prey, but there wasn't much meat on the bone. Even loaded with low speed, low mass ammo, her gun was too strong. You can't skin and gut a pink-misted animal. "Knife hunting it is, then," she said to herself with a twisted grin. She drew a double-bladed knife with a bone handle from a sheath on her thigh and tested the edge. She purred with pleasure at its smooth, clean feel.

The sun was low by the time she found her way back to camp. She had a sack full of voracious, aggressive rodent monsters intending nasty terror. She could already smell Priest's culinary experiments. "Pork," she wondered, sampling the air, tasting barbecue on the wind. "I hope he found some spam or tiny weenies in his pack after all?" Priest and his minister were at their usual bickering, but there were other voices as well.

Rounding a corner, she saw Priest's minister's guts pouring in coils from a wide, angry gash across his belly. His face was placid and serene as he stapled his body back together. Priest watched on, testy and arrogant as ever as he waited for his man to patch himself up.

What stunned Gracie was that towering over Priest were four war boars. Massive and ugly, they rumbled, eyes blazing with internal fury and LED light. Her eyes traveled up the flanks of the beasts and saw their riders sitting high in saddles, tall and lean. Each one wore custom armor and a mask glittering with optical devices. A bundle of cords and cables linked the passengers to their mounts, from mask to skull. The boars and their riders all snapped their attention to her in horrifying unison.

The rider on the eldest boar, bristles white with age, wielded a massive compound bow. He had aimed at Priest's heart, but with no loss in accuracy it found its mark on Gracie's left eye. She dropped her sack of varmints and drew her pistol on the bowman's mask. "Priest," she said, "what's going on here? What do these gentlemen," she looked over at the riders and corrected herself when she came to the end of the line. "And lady want?"

"Oh good," he snapped. "You're back. And late for stew. I would offer you some but gutless here had to have seconds." He looked back at the beast riders almost as if he had forgotten about them. "Oh, and these guys. They appeared about a minute or so after you'd left and we've all been waiting on you. They're here to take us to the Walking Sisters."

"You sure," she asked. "They're not what I was expecting." She had the bowman dead in her sights and with a twitch of her finger he could be buzzard food. If anyone was offering directions she figured it would be out of kindness, not coercion. There was something a little too on the nose about these guys.

The other three boars circled around, rumbling, growling and drooling. A rider in heavy crimson armor on a boar with matching bristles drew a long broadsword. Its steel was a swirling black and red pattern like flames climbing its edge. The third rider wore beetle black armor on a jet-black war boar and hefted a massive battle ax. Their sister-in-arms, the final rider, already had her weapon out. Her long, cruel-looking scythe was still dripping with the minister's blood. She rode bare-chested with large, crude cross hairs tattooed across her bosom.

"No," Priest sighed. "They're fine. Lower your gun. These are the messengers the Sisters send when it's time for a meeting." He spat into the dirt. "Ok, come on," he waved his hands, "everyone here is friendly, we don't need to immolate, disembowel or impale anyone else! Let's all calm down for 30 seconds, we'll pass the," he looked into his stew pot and shuddered, "food," he concluded.

"Tell your Praetorian to lower her weapon," the White Rider ordered.

"Priest, my trigger finger is itchy," Gracie warned.

"Damn it, Gracie, gun down," Priest roared. "These people do not mess around!"

"Neither do I," Gracie said. Her target's forehead was in line with her reticule. She was only loaded for small game, but a shot between the eyes would knock them from their saddle. Then a knife between the ribs or up under the armpit would keep them down.

"Gracie," Priest now said and, voice above a whisper, "you need to trust me on this. Put," he stepped towards her, "your gun," he laid his hand on the barrel, "down."

Gracie Caer allowed herself to look into Priest's eyes and recognized the truth, or at least the urgency. She took a deep breath and relaxed her finger from the trigger, lowering her gun. "Alright," she said. "The gun is down." She looked from one masked face to the next.

She relaxed, and the white rider before her, muscles tensed and ready to fire, vanished. The other three riders relaxed, sheathing their respective weapons. "What," Gracie stammered. "Where," searching for the phantom target that stood before her with murderous intent. She stepped back and felt the stinking furnace breath of a war boar pour down her shoulders. She jumped, glaring hard from the beady red eyes of the boar, then to the impassive lenses of the rider's mask. "Cheap trick," she grumbled.

The white rider kept his bow flexed for a moment longer, but at last relaxed. "It is well," he said.

"Now," Priest said, straightening his jacket, "we are all impressed. You eviscerated my minister and got the drop on my Praetorian. You said you were emissaries from the Walking Sisters? They know that I've been looking for them?"

"We are the Harbingers," the Pale Rider said. "They know you seek them and have invited you to join them."

"All three of you are to attend," the Red Rider continued. "But you must leave all your weapons and possessions behind."

"Hold up now," Gracie said, holding a hand up. "I leave my guns for nobody."

"You will leave them," the Black Rider warned, "or you can count this as the end of your journey." All four boars rumbled louder and advanced a step.

"Nope, nope, it's all good," Priest laughed. Sweat coursed down his face as he tossed weapons, bandoliers and satchels to the ground. "Gods damn it, Gracie, these cats do not mess around," he hissed at her. "Drop it all or we're all boar food!" Gracie kept glaring, outraged by the small mountain of supplies growing at Priest's feet.

"Where was this grit when we were digging those corpses from the lab," she threw her hands up in frustration. "Fine. Fine," she snarled, "and if any of these pieces go missing, you are paying to replace it!" She dropped her long gun first, followed by her sidearm. Then a collection of throwing knives, stars and darts hit the ground in rapid succession. She pulled a machete from the scabbard on her back and a hefty fighting knife emerged from her boot. The last of her equipment, a long, curved kukri slid from its sheath on her hip. She kissed it and laid it upon the ground.

The Pale Rider looked at the Black Rider, then back at Gracie, a sly smile spread across her black lips. "Everything," she said, rolling her hand at the wrist.

Gracie glared. "Oh, bloody fine," she pouted and pulled one last snub-nosed revolver from her other boot and added it to the pile. "That's everything! Satisfied?" She crossed her arms and stuck out her lower lip.

"That will do. For now," said the Red Rider. "We will no doubt have to do a second check once we meet the Sisters."

"Now what," the minister asked, toying with the staples in his belly.

"Now," the White Rider announced, "let's start our journey. You three can join my companions on the ride. We have a long way to go, and we should make haste." Priest rode alongside the Red Rider, noticing the unique scent of the boar. His minister sat next to the Black Rider, while Gracie rode with the Pale Rider. Being closer now, they could admire the intricate details on their escorts' armor. The Red Rider wore sturdy crimson plate mail with elegant patterns, looking impenetrable. The White Rider's armor was made of flexible snowy-white chainmail and leather. The Black Rider sported matte ebony scale mail. The Pale Rider wore black leather leggings and a breechcloth. She showed her strength and skill, in contrast to the others. Her body bore scars and tattoos from a lifetime of battles, her hair shone in the light with vibrant colors.

"Onward," the White Rider called, "You have questions, and they must have answers!"

The red sun hung low with golden radiant beams, showing them their road. The Walking Sisters waited beyond the trees, offering wisdom and guidance, but no hope.

***

One
Night

Eagles
Met in the
Indigo dark clouds;
Nobody saw them circling.
Down below in vaults of the damned, three travelers rest
Basing camp in hidden test labs
Eager for some sleep
They got none.
Worst night.
Eat
Eggs.
Not now.
The Sisters
Have sent their best four
Riders on pigs to collect them.
Even now, as I ride this flock of little black birds
Eyes in the sky, fly right behind
Stalk them, spy on them.
Eat roadkill.
Night sweat.
Tick.
Tock.
Hold up;
Eyes don't fail,
Riders have caught up
Isolated and all alone,
Defenseless in the open wastes, they choose to follow.
Eager cavalry whisk them off,
Race by the river
Search for camp
Fly on.
Out.
Up.
Race on
Forever,
Or at least until
Recon bodies find our target.

Must find Eurydice by any means possible.
Even if it means possessing
Friends and family.
Or children.
Reason
Must
Yield
Facts and
Argue for
The logical end.
Eurydice or death, I fear.
To be clear, I cannot deceive myself about this
Our fate is sealed if we lose hope.
Stay strong, one more time.
Easy peas.
Easy.

Chapter 14

The three travelers rode into a little camp, their arms and backs screaming in stiff pain. Priest gripped the plates in the Red rider's armor, his eyes reading over the details in the inlay. His minister with the Black rider, one arm around the rider's waist, the other clutching his belly. Gracie held onto the Pale rider's torso, seeing now her host's chest wrapped in a tight, stained bandeau. The White rider led, following an unseen path through stunted trees and rocks. "We are here," he announced, bringing the group to a stop.

Caravans of varying upkeep sat in a horseshoe around a bonfire. A metalworker collaborated with a tech artist, threading circuitry into weapons and machines. An alchemist watched the newcomers from behind her still. Screams and the ratcheting of power tools burst from a third caravan. Someone painted a red cross across the front. The next semicircle of caravans sat around a final caravan. This last wagon sat unadorned except for three large eyes painted across the front door.

"There," the White rider pointed to the eye. "You go in. They have been waiting for you."

"Oh good," Priest said, sliding from his mount without an ounce of grace. "Any chance we can get a ride back to our camp when this is over?" He looked from the White rider to the Black, but their masked faces revealed nothing.

"That depends," the Pale rider said as Gracie dismounted, doing her best to keep her hands to herself. "It depends on what the Sisters instruct us to do when your time is up." Her mask revealed nothing. The way its visual sensors tracked Gracie made her uncomfortable. "Go on," she said. "They don't like to wait."

The caravan's interior was velvet dark, lit by a constellation of console displays. Lights glowed through dense clouds of incense and dried herbs. Screens and cables cannibalized from dozens of sources occupied every empty space. Three women, identical triplets, sat on a threadbare purple couch. They passed a hookah between themselves, exhaling plumes of thick, sweet-smelling smoke. Their masks, like those of the war boar riders, linked each woman to the other two in a complex network of cables. They wore black three-piece suits tricked out with fine red lining. Their suits, rumpled and stained from travel, bore an air of formality Priest did not expect. Their socks were also red, matching their suit lining. Their shoes shone with a spotless mirror polish.

"You've finally come," the Central Sister said at long last, exhaling a plume of smoke. "We were expecting you sooner."

"You come seeking guidance," the Left Sister said, her voice identical to the middle.

"Many come for guidance, wisdom, fortunes," the Right Sister said. "What you walk away with depends on yourselves. *Caveat Emptor*[14]."

"The buyer determines value, not the seller," Priest smiled, enjoying a power game. "But we have not had introductions, and I can't know if we will be receiving an accurate reading until I am satisfied."

The sister in the middle pursed her lips and held out her hand. The sister on the left handed her a small box made of black sandalwood. "We save these for our more pedestrian visitors," she said, "but for you they may hold some meaning." She removed a deck of cards and shuffled them before placing a single card before each of the travelers. "Flip them," she said, "and know yourselves as we know you."

Degory Priest, his minister and Praetorian Gracie Caer all flipped their cards. Before Priest stood the tower card. The minister drew the hanged man bound upon a scaffold. Gracie

---

[14] Let the buyer beware.

only saw Death. "I suppose this is all well and good for parlor games," Priest sniffed. "But I came here for a hint of clarity."

"Of course," the sister on the right said now. "We've seen it all before. You opened a box and let something out. You aren't the only party seeking it."

"In that, you will fail, Priest," said the sister in the middle. "What you let out isn't from this time or this place. It does not follow the rules of our world and it cannot be bound by the constructs of any who walk this plain." She inhaled smoke from the hookah and exhaled. "Even you are powerless to catch it, Priest," she said.

"If you want advice," the sister on the left said, "go to where it is going. Find what, or whom, it is looking for, and deal with the consequences of your actions."

"But be quick," the central sister chimed in, "you aren't the only one zeroing in upon its destination. You have attracted attention to your quarry, to yourself, to our very existence."

Priest tugged at his collar. Sweat flowed down the curve of Gracie's back. She attempted to stifle a cough but it came, nonetheless. It caught in her throat and she choked upon it.

"You look tired," the right sister observed. "Sit and rest now. There are things you must hear now that you may understand now, later, or never at all." Behind them, three chairs of lacquered black wood and red leather swirled into being.

"Don't be too surprised," the sister on the left smiled. "Here, in our home, things are how we want them to be and how we perceive them to be." She gestured to a bowl of fruit that had not been there before. "Eat," she said, "you will need your strength for what comes next." None of the fleshy objects were of any familiar shape or color, but they appeared ripe and smelled sweet. Priest handed something the size of his fist with seven ridges to his minister. It was the color of bruised twilight.

"Take a bite and tell me if it's poisonous," he said, whispering.

The three hostesses watched them, their ruby-red eyepieces unblinking in the dim light. "I don't believe our guests seek comfort, sister," the triplet on the right said. "Let us proceed to the business at hand."

"Oh, how dull," the central sibling sniffed. She reached into a pocket inside her suit jacket and produced a tarnished silver lighter. She gave it an experimental flick before tossing it to Gracie. "Be a dear," the sibling on the left said, "and light the candles for us?"

The fruit was gone, but now a half dozen candles circled the space around them. Gracie lifted an eyebrow to Priest who nodded, and he lit the candles. Warm, flickering light dominated the room. The central sister collected the three cards and returned them to her sandalwood box. "Now," she said, looking at the minister, "you. Stand before us."

The minister gulped and looked to Priest for direction. His Adeptus rolled his hand at the wrist, signaling he got on with it. He sighed and stood before the three sisters.

"Open your shirt," the sister on the left ordered.

"Priest," he whimpered. "Sir, I'm getting uncomfortable with this."

"Oh, for the love of," Priest snapped. "Open up your damn shirt like the lady said."

The minister sighed again and opened up his shirt. Yards and yards of filthy electrical tape kept his angry, puckered gash bound. With a nimble flick of her wrist, the sister on the right sliced through the tape with a gleaming butterfly knife. He looked down as his bowels once again spilled out onto his feet before the weird sisters. "Gods damn it all," he muttered as the three women leaned in closer to examine the pink and purple tissues, "I had everything back where I wanted them." They whispered among themselves as they gleaned the future from the coils of his guts.

"You will do well to stay together," the central sister finally said, loud enough for them to hear. "But you have some important decisions ahead of you." She drew from her hookah stem and exhaled sweet smelling smoke. "Choose well," she said.

"You will do well to stay together," the sister on the right agreed. "Continue on your path to good fortune," she continued.

Priest and Gracie both watched with disgusted fascination.

The central sister gasped and held a hand to her mouth. "Priest, you will receive a great shock," she nodded to the minister's open belly. "A greater shock, but it will halt your progress." She shuffled deeper into the minister's body cavity and smiled. "I do not see your mission ending, yet."

"Thank you, minister," the sister on the right said at last, "I would say we have seen everything you can show us." She reached into the darkness behind her couch and produced a large stapler. "Please coil and patch yourself up."

"There is more you must learn," the sister on the left said. The middle sister filled a fresh bowl for their hookah with a sweet-smelling sticky resin. "Unfortunately for you, no one can tell you what you must learn" she gave a cryptic smile. "You will have to see it for yourselves."

Priest accepted the offered hookah stem, trying to not touch his minister's blood. Gracie and his minister also breathed in the hot, chemical smoke. Their eyelids grew heavy and everything felt distant. Smoke grew thick like old suede, shimmering in greens, magentas and purples. Patterns formed and tessellated, breaking apart and reforming into a dozen fractal patterns. Curtains of dense smoke parted and they found themselves elsewhere, in a place that wasn't a place. A brilliant light shown down from high above upon a wooden stage. A true Brechtian space spread around them.

A massive stag and a dire wolf circled each other on the stage. The stag pawed the stage and a low growl boiled from the wolf's throat. In a flash they were on each other, teeth to throat and antlers to underbelly. The fight was savage but brief and in the end both beasts lay dead on the stage in a spreading pool of blood. The stag and wolf collapsed upon each other, replaced by a squid and whale grappling in a death grip. Tentacles lashed, jaws snapped and clouds of black ink swirled around, engulfing everything.

The clouds of ink parted and a golden eagle clutching an emerald serpent in its claws soared above them. The eagle's beak snapped upon the serpent's throat and it shrieked in pain as needle fangs tore into its throat. The combatants savaged each other and merged one last time, fused into a fearsome hybrid.

It bore no known shape and curled upon itself in some places while it billowed out in others. Appendages grew and formed, folding back into itself, rolling inside out.

Beyond the few physical details they could agree upon, none of them could describe what they saw. Somewhere deep in the mass, a face swam to the surface. Its mouth spread beyond the capacity of a human jaw's reach in an endless scream from beyond time and space.

Before the last vaporous fingers of consciousness receded, a final voice came through. "While you go about your quest," it was the sisters, but all three speaking at once, "keep an eye out for brother," she said. "He might help you. They might not. It depends. It depends on so much," she said. It was one voice, but Priest heard it three times. "They are the Walking Brothers, but they are the Cerberus. They are the hounds that guard the gates of Hell."

The baying of many beasts split the silence.

***

Early daylight and the chattering of morning birds pierced through Degory Priest's restless sleep. Bit by bit and pound by pound he felt his body wake, cramped, nauseous and out of joint but at least awake. His bodyguard Gracie Caer lay nearby as did his anonymous lout of a Minister. He focused on the blurry shapes, and they snapped into clarity. The three of them had been abandoned at their original camp. Their mounted escort even stole from their limited supplies, demanding payment for their troubles.

"Gracie," he called. She did not wake up at first. He threw a rock at her boot.

Gracie Caer snorted and rolled over on the cold pavement. She didn't know her sleeping mat was among the yet unlisted missing items.

Priest took his time standing, feeling every kink in every joint and every knot in every muscle as he did so. "Gracie," he said again, "time to get up. We need to get walking." He assessed the damages. He concluded that, if they didn't find food and water, their journey would end soon. "They took all our food, Gracie," he said.

That woke her up. "What," she demanded, "do you mean they took all our food?" She still had her weapons, may the Sisters of the Slaughter be praised, but this was their food. "You're telling me that after kidnapping and drugging us, they took all our food? Everything?"

"That sums it up," Priest said, now kicking his Minister awake. "Maybe hunt us up some grub while I figure out our next step?"

The four riders had indeed taken all their food, water and medicine. They were kind enough to leave some sleeping gear and a few other items and toiletries. But, by Gracie's count they had three days before things got desperate.

"Guess I'm hunting," Gracie grunted. "Again. Do me a favor, Priest, and have a plan by the time I get back." She put her precious blades away. Then, she loaded a fresh magazine into her gun and stormed off into the bracken.

Shadows bent and the sun hung low in the west by the time Gracie returned. The hunt provided less this time with only a trio of malnourished spine puppies in a sack as her only reward. Priest and his Minister had scrawled a quarter mile of proofs down the sunbleached old road. By the broken, dehydrated nature of their screaming and their purple faces, their disagreement was bitter.

"For N'yarlat-Hotep's sake," Priest spat, "we've been over these equations three times. The outcome resonance will put us within 25 kilometers of our target." He looked at the chalk figures on the ground. "For the most part," he concluded.

"You're forgetting that three of us are going through the aperture," his Minister replied. "And all three of us are expecting to come out on the other side." He pointed to a string of algebra written in three different languages. "You know the only certainty comes from the mass of a single individual. That being me," he said, "since I was the one you sent through for each of your tests."

"We had to calibrate it somehow," Degory pointed out, "and we got the bugs corrected," Priest returned, "through trial and error."

"Most of the errors being the exit aperture closes before I'm all the way through. I know I'll be fine in time, but what happens if your minder gets trapped between apertures? What happens if you do?"

"I mean, if she gets stuck, that's what she gets paid for," Priest waved the idea off. "She's a professional bullet sponge. And if I don't make it, well then end of story, sorry, Sally."

"And then I'm stuck wandering forever," the Minister hissed. "Long after the last human. Long after the last animal. Long after the sun winks out!"

"Oh, please," Priest said, "stop making everything about you."

"So what are you two aunties nipping at each other over," Gracie decided now was the best time to interrupt. She tossed the spine puppies on the ground by their fire. Then, she sat on a log and filled a fresh pipe. It had been a fruitless day of hunting for less than vermin to eat. "Remember, this is the best meal we'll get for a long time." She took a luxuriant inhale and said, "So, whatever your plan is, these scrappers had better be enough to get us there."

"Simply put," Priest pontificated, "teleportation."

"Don't even think about it," his Minister warned.

"We've got some of my experimental equipment with us," Priest pressed on, "and my tests were promising."

"You could barely make it work twice under controlled conditions," the Minister said.

Priest growled, "Like our huntress said, we're out of food. We can't keep going for another day, let alone three weeks to reach Orevada on the *Obscura res15*' path." He said, "Here's what I think: we can cut the distance. Check this out," he added, pulling out a small rocket from his bag and held it up. "We can use this to get there faster. Skip the miles of war boars, surface eels and scorpion-crabs. We launch this baby with the right coordinates and we'll step right through a doorway from here to there! Easy as that!"

"Except," the Minister pushed in, "as I've alluded to, we've never sent more than one person through for all our test runs. We don't know how that will translate, if the threshold will maintain for long enough, if we'll be on the right continent. The list of risks is too long for me to agree to this."

"And we'll take your worry into consideration," Priest said, already prepping the tiny missile with his coordinates. "All I know is we've wasted enough time, energy and resources to get this far."

"Why don't we raid the Weird Sisters," Gracie asked. "It should be easy enough to find their camp and retrieve our gear."

"If only it were so easy," Priest laughed. "You go ahead and retrace our path. Even if you could find the hollow where they had their campers, I'll bet you solid they're long gone. It's how they are. You don't find them. They find you. And then they're gone. Now," he said, "are there any more objections or misplaced worries before we kick my plan into gear?"

"You already decided it's what you want to do," his Minister said, defeated. "Let's get this over with. But don't say I didn't warn you."

Priest fine-tuned the rocket's settings then primed the engine. He set it down and ran once a fierce chemical reaction in the fuel cell erupted with a blinding blue-white flame from the tail, launching it into the sky, beyond sight.

---

[15] Dark thing's

Gracie witnessed the spectacle, awestruck, shielding her eyes as the rocket pierced the sky. She nearly jumped out of her boots when the air before her rippled and distorted like a powerful heat wave. She saw unfamiliar buildings and landscapes in fleeting glimpses. They were far from the dense, weed-choked thickets of the lowlands. Electricity crackled, and she was transported to mountains, desert, and the ruins of an unknown city. The next instant, she was back on the fractured highway amidst her camping gear. The wind intensified as the desert landscape solidified before her. The pungent smell of ozone mixed with a thousand other odors choked Gracie. Tears streamed down her face. But, she couldn't look away from the reality-bending spectacle unfolding before her.

"Alright," Priest shouted, grabbing his Minister and Gracie by their elbows, "it's now or never time!" He ululated a wild, shrieking yelp to the skies and dragged his companions into the rift before them. "*Videbo te in alteram partem*[16]*!*"

---

[16] I'll see you on the other side.

Chapter 15

Murdoc's Rest. Three years ago. Gracie had led her legions well with an army of some 50,000 troops, including infantry, cavalry, and artillery. They chased her quarry, a detachment of anti-imperial separatists, in a four-day campaign that had been successful at picking off the stragglers, but the main body was just too fast. The quarry had fled into the protection of the rocks and crags along a steep, hook-shaped ridge. Gracie monitored her battalions through field glasses and ordered final adjustments to her commanders. The rattle of gunfire peppered the air, punctuated by the distant booms of cannon fire. Multicolored tracer rounds streaked the twilight in both directions.

"Keep the big guns focused to the eastern ridge," she called out to her artillery commanders. "I want them staring into the sun when we rush them with the cavalry." Distant rumbles and a faint, hot breeze greeted her, shifting her hair in its wake. The sky glowed red with bonfires stoked with the bodies of the slain. Towers of black, greasy smoke marked the sky. Gracie closed her eyes and took a deep breath.

"Lieutenant General Caer," a runner approached, hand raised in salute. "We've got all companies surrounding the hostiles. We're keeping them pinned up on the ridge between the cavalry and artillery gunners. Infantry battalions are keeping the holes closed but they're itching to get in there."

Gracie smiled. This campaign had been hard fought up until now. The first half of the week, her mission was fresh and a roller coaster of anxiety and excitement. Once spotted, the chase was on. The anti-imperialists had the head start but Gracie's army ate up the stragglers as they caught up. She chastised herself and punished her subordinates for letting their prey take refuge. But, this would also make her victory sweeter.

"Sun is starting to go down," Gracie told the runner. "Spread the word we hold the line for tonight. Nobody gets in or out. Keep the artillery hitting them often. And make sure the pony boys stop escapees." She dismissed the runner. But, she called him back, saying, "tell everyone we should have this done before lunch tomorrow."

Contritium praecedit superbia[17].

Gracie's arrogance led to the slaughter of thousands of her best infantry the next morning. Disease swept through her camp, killing many and weakening countless others, despite her medics' tireless efforts. The gunfire from above had subsided, and Gracie sneered; her forces had killed a few rebels, but at a bloody cost. The treacherous terrain leading to the foothills slowed her advance, and snipers and light artillery picked off more of her troops. Undeterred, she drove them forward, convinced they would soon crush their enemies and claim the ridge.

She could no longer hear, except for a chorus of agony intertwined with ecstasy. Soldiers trained and conditioned since childhood called for mothers who would never come. Parties on both sides sang discordant battle hymns while swords and knives crashed against armored plates and bullets punctuated their arguments with bitter ellipsis. She saw nothing but red, crimson, scarlet, claret and copper. She screamed with furious joy until the fibers in her larynx tore, though she could feel the scratchy, frail keening that replaced her ferocious battle cry.

In this moment, Gracie Caer was War, embodiment of Mars, avatar of Ares, the shieldmaiden of Tyr. An electric cocktail of adrenaline and battle drugs surged through her blood and she couldn't stop moving if she wanted to.

With a sudden jolt, the world went black and she was no longer any of those things. In the midst of her charge, in the midst of her warriors racing alongside her with the thunder of

---

[17] Grief before pride.

guns and the roar of cannons ringing in her ears, one chance blow, a single coincidental meeting of slag with skull felled her into deep comatose sleep before she could take another step.

At the end of the conflict, Gracie woke up to find herself chained in the middle of a clearing littered with the remains of battle, surrounded by separatists. The fallen lay entangled, their bodies were broken and charred. Their uniforms were so caked with mud and gore that it was impossible to tell the opposing sides apart. It would take a full week for her to be returned to her superiors, courtesy of a begrudging ransom. She would learn this during her tribunal and court martial. She had not, as she thought, ousted the traitors from their stronghold. Instead, she had unwittingly led seven of her nine battalions to ruin. With the loss of 30,000 troops, all killed, wounded, or listed as missing, the Empire's efforts to consolidate the Balkanized territory came to a bitter halt.

Due to her rank and esteem, the former Lieutenant General would be spared execution or imprisonment, but rather endure the humiliation of having her rank and titles stripped away. She had no one to blame but herself.

O quomodo ceciderunt fortes[18].

***

In the beginning, there was nothing. No time, no space, not even the void held in the spaces between the smallest of things. Darkness gave way to pale, pasty light, and the only physical sensation was pain. Mass became tissue and tissue became organs. Someone groaned but neither party could decide who did it yet. The meat pile thought it was being stabbed in the chest but came to terms with its own heartbeat. Twin blurs of light and shadow combined and form returned to the world, and shapes took meaning. Its voice was husky and dry as it wiped drool from its swollen, puffy lips. "I taste metal."

---

[18] Oh how the mighty have fallen

Priest had been awake for hours since they came through. He had more than enough time to get a small fire going, eat his share of rations and have a pipe. Once finished, he stood up, sauntered over and kicked Gracie in the ribs. "Wakey wakey," he rumbled, "eggs and bakey."

Gracie groaned. "Goddamnit so much, Devil Man," she whined. "Give a girl a moment to collect herself after she's been through a quantum scrambler." She rubbed her eyes and her vision finally tracked, "how long have I been out," she asked.

"Long enough," Priest said, gazing across the wilderness with a pair of binoculars. "My gambit worked. We're about a day's walk from Orevada now, but it's not going to be easy." He handed her the field glasses.

Priest struck camp in a mountain pass by the side of a desert road. A few carrion birds wheeled high above under sullen gunmetal clouds. Blast craters full of broken war machines and countless bones pitted the land. "Sweet, steaming shit," Priest breathed, "is it wrong that I am a little jealous?"

Gracie looked around, now aware that they were down a party member. "Where's your Minister," she demanded. "You launched your bottle rocket. Everything went all funhouse mirror," she wiped her mouth. "I could vomit everything from the base of my colon up." She went down hard on her knees and heaved.

"Yeah." Priest watched with a mix of amusement and interest. Ropes of thick mucus dripped from her nose and mouth. "The old silly-nanny was right to worry about one thing, at least. He didn't make it."

Gracie glared up at him with puffy red eyes and naked anger. "Didn't make it, what's that mean," she asked.

"He didn't make it, I'm not sure how much more clear you need me to be." Priest gave her a hand once she felt ready to stand again. He looked into her eyes, frowned and sniffed the air near her neck, detecting a whiff of acetone, but shook his head. "There was no question I was going to make it. I wasn't sure if you would survive the condensation process, but here we, well, you and I, are."

Gracie brushed her sweaty hair back and glared at the same blurry horizon Priest gazed upon. "What's that mean for him," she croaked.

"The full explanation is too long and full of tangents," Priest said, seeking out hope for life. "The short answer is he's going to have some difficulties returning to all three dimensions." Priest grimaced. "Imagine a water balloon full of blood and ground beef expanding at the speed of light from a singularity. Imagine it expanding so fast and the balloon expands beyond its limits and pops. Now imagine the second it pops, time reverses and the blood and meat return to the balloon. The balloon shrinks back to the singularity, only to expand, explode, and continue the cycle."

Gracie looked at Priest with eyes full of terror. "And then all that's left of him is a puddle and chunks," she asked, incredulous.

"No, it's worse," Priest said. "During tests, the cycle frequency was so fast we needed special cameras to observe it. Within seconds, entropy caught up with him, causing his cycle of exploding and reforming to slow, until he reverted back to his original state." Priest puffed out his cheeks and whistled. "When I asked him how it went from his perspective, he told me each rapid cycle lasted hours. He felt himself swell, tear apart, explode, then smash back down again to do it over and over."

"He's got a lot to look forward to," Gracie shuddered.

Priest smiled. "You have no idea," he said.

Orevada was a row of black, broken teeth in the distance. Smoke rose in high columns here and there, darkening the already bruised sky. Farming communities and water reclamation towers lay burnt and broken. Priest looked back and forth, trying to find evidence of life amid the wreckage and then stopped.

"What is it," Gracie asked, grabbing the binoculars, "what do you see?"

"The Wild Hunt is still on here," Priest whispered, "at least some of the celebrants of the Frenzy are still here." Far below, in the wreckage, two tiny shapes that could be mistaken for humans lurked in the wreckage. Few had ever encountered the Wild Hunt and lived to tell about it. A tsunami of slaughter swept up and consumed almost any and all survivors.

"They didn't stand a chance," Gracie said. "They had towers, gun posts," she paused, squinting once more through the field glasses. "Roadblocks. Bleeding shit, they got them all!" She could see a few figures lurking amidst the wreckage but they were too far away to pick out specifics.

She increased the zoom and looked closer at the devastation on the horizon. Bombed out buildings with shattered windows like blind eyes leaned everywhere. Blackened streaks of soot or blood stained cracked walls. A brief motion or glint of light on the edge of her peripheral vision still didn't sit right with her.

"I don't think we're alone," Gracie Caer whispered, tracing the wreckage along the wall.

"What makes you say that," Priest asked.

"I'm seeing signs," she said. "It's not like the Wild Hunt to clean up after themselves. They're like rabid war boars. They'll tear a place to absolute pieces and leave a big smear across the landscape everywhere they go." She spat in disgust, "anyone who gets caught up in their frenzy gets transformed; what once was is no more."

"Well," Priest said, getting up, "what are we waiting for?"

"What the hell are you doing," Gracie grabbed his shoulder and shoved him down hard. "If there are two shamblers down there, you can bet your kidneys there are more!"

"The joke's on you," Priest sneered. "I can get more," he eyed up the small of her back, "but if Eurydice is out nearby, we are getting her out. That was the deal."

"That was the deal," Gracie said, "but, if we don't find her by sundown tonight, I am gone, understood? I don't like being as close to the Wild Hunt as we are!"

Adeptus Priest and his Praetorian kept to the shadows, scuttling between rubble piles. For brief, fleeting moments, the nightmare forms passed into the light. They were lurking in the tangle of collapse. "Take this," Gracie said, passing him one of her fighting knives. "*Habere melius est quam egere19.*" It wasn't her kukri, but it was long, sharp and serrated on one side. Its weight was reassuring in his hand.

Gracie peered around a shattered brick wall, guns drawn. Priest peered around the opposite side. One or two Celebrants would be easy enough to take down, for sure. But if they were too slow or loud the Great Hunt would descend upon their heads in exponential fury.

This was how it always went.

"On the count of three," Gracie whispered, "we are running to that two-story structure ahead of us, got it?" Priest nodded, eyes wide, jaw tense, knuckles flexing. "Don't trip, because I am not coming back for you! If they catch you, I'll put one between your eyes, but that's the only favor you'll get, see?" Priest nodded.

"Alright. On three," she repeated. He tensed, brow furrowed. "One," she licked her lips, sweat beading on her forehead. "Two." The count landed like an executioner's drumbeat. "Three."

***

"She was here," Priest hissed, slapping Cassandra's shoulder, "look!" The building was a shell, a burnt out husk with most of the roof missing. In one corner, they found a sleeping pad and food tins. In the other, math graffiti covered the whole wall. It told a tale of stubborn survival. Equipment lay scattered about in various states of repair on the floor. There were bloodstains everywhere.

"This could be from anyone," Gracie said, "any lone survivor could have holed up in here a spell. It's dry, secure and if you don't put a light on or make a lot of noise, it's discrete." Gracie peeked inside a trashed vestibule that served

---

[19] To have is better than to need.

as a washroom and gagged. A razorblade salad of knives, black and crusty with blood filled the filthy sink under a mirror.

Priest stabbed his finger at the arcane formulae covering the walls. "First, only Eurydice is wily enough to survive this level of torment," Priest said. "If she could survive me, she could survive an insane amount of self-surgery, but those proofs confirm it's her." He grinned.

"How can you be sure," Gracie said, "it came from one of her nerd friends." There was a logic to the characters to be sure, cryptic beyond any means of Gracie's understanding.

"These signify coordinates for a teleporter beacon," Priest read through the numbers. "At one point she must have tried to launch a rocket, but there must have been a problem. Something must have stopped her," he said. He frowned, staring at the cryptic spaghetti and muttered to himself.

"You mean there are more than one of those whizbangs out there," Gracie said. "I don't know how you can stand to travel like that," she rubbed her neck and back, "I still feel like I've been through a ringer."

Priest shone the light into her eyes. "Oh my," he hissed, "it's happening to you a lot faster than I anticipated!"

"What," Gracie grabbed his wrist in an iron grip, squinting against the penlight. "Is happening faster than you anticipated?" The pain in the base of her neck was creeping its way up the back of her skull into her temples.

"Nothing, nothing," Priest gasped. "We only stopped existing when I translated our mass to energy as we entered the portal. Then, we came out and made crude facsimiles." He laughed, sweat pouring down his forehead. "So at least we know Eurydice was here," he tried to take his wrist back, but her grip only tightened further.

"Wait," Gracie grabbed his face in her hands, drawing him close until their noses touched. "So you're telling me we're DEAD?" Her breath was hot and angry.

"Well," Priest stuttered, "you didn't think it was like walking through a door to another room, did you? Yes. Your original body is dead and gone, less than vapor. We are soulless abominations that fill the void of where our original bodies once trod. It buys us time to finish off what we started before these temporary meat sacks start to break down." He gulped. "My tech can map our neural pathways and genetic structure only so well. You must have noticed a memory lapse or two by now?"

"You didn't tell me any of this," Gracie hissed, teeth grinding. She could feel his skull creaking between her hands, "how long do we have?"

"It's hard to say," Priest gasped. "I've only done preliminary experiments with my minister who is," he waved his hand in the air, "gone. He would collapse into a dissolute organic puddle after a week. He would lose his hair first, then his skin would slough off like an old bathrobe, then," tears were forming in his eyes. "His bones crumbled to nothing. But then he got better."

"So," Gracie said, staring daggers into his soul, "we have a week before we crumble into dust?"

"If we're lucky," Priest said, "now if you would stop being so whiny, can we please focus on the task at hand?"

Gracie released him and punched her fist into a brick wall. She felt her knuckles go off like a series of gunshots, and blood soaked her hand. "You son of a bitch," she muttered.

"We can discuss my mother's failings later," Priest said, trying to read further into Eurydice's notes. "There is a message here, code that will tell us where she moved on to, where her next camp may be." His brow furrowed, and he whispered more syllables to himself as he traced images to the symbols. "Tah-dow," he announced, pointing out a final set of figures, "coordinates. We can at least find where she went to next, but this is all very, very strange," he mused.

"Why is that," Gracie asked, rubbing her hand, sucking the blood from her singing fingers.

"She didn't use her teleporter to fast-blast her way out of here," he said. "More's the better because that would make all this the more urgent, but," he rubbed his chin, "she's sticking around. She is still in the vicinity of Orevada for some reason."

"Then we'll have to ask her when we find her," Gracie said, pulling out her guns once more. "Come on, Priest, we're burning daylight." She stomped away, swearing under her breath.

The sky had gone overcast since they had been inside covering the world in a hematite dome. Every few yards, Gracie pulled Priest behind concrete slabs and flipped vehicles. She heard footsteps down every corridor and saw impossible shadows around every corner.

"We're getting close now," he said after she dragged him into the belly of a burnt-out tank. Priest poked at the carbonized remains of the crew still plastered to the walls. It smelled of old, cold barbecue and spent matches.

"Good," Gracie whispered, peering through cracked view ports. "Because I am getting the creeps something fierce here."

They crept past silent pickets and empty foxholes, pausing to smell the air or listen to silence. Traps and minefields forced them to double back and find new paths. Gracie looked at the contrasting imagery with unease. Priest's mind was elsewhere. Here and there he found items mixed into the rubble. Ration wrappers, shell casings, and small strips of cloth stood out like flood lights. "She's left us a trail," he exclaimed, "her next camp should be in one of these buildings!"

"Priest," Gracie said, looking at the arterial spray of graffiti covering a wall. "Does any of this look familiar to you?"

The Adeptus Physicus poked his head from a pile of rubble and saw the world around him. Now he was aware of the signs all around him; posters, spray paint, and corpses clad in eclectic armor. Cadaverous brick-a-brack cluttered everywhere. Only an expert could separate the city guards from the Wild Hunters.

"They told me nothing of this when they briefed me about Orevada's fall," Gracie said. "There was nothing about Emperor Norton." She pulled a poster from the wall with three lines slashed across it in jagged strokes of paint:

UNA OMNIUM DEMENTIA EST, UNA INSANIA CUNCTIS
FURIOSUS FURORE SUO PUNITOR
IRA FUROR BREVIS EST[20]

None of this was familiar to either of them; none of this bade well for either of them. "We need to leave," Gracie Caer said, backing away, "now."

"I agree one hundred percent," Priest replied, not enjoying the graphic imagery.

They turned, both of them now aware of footsteps immediately behind them. Two celebrants of the Wild Hunt approached. Deformed with infectious madness and self-inflicted injuries they shrieked and attacked.

"Shit." Gracie hissed through her teeth, and shoved Priest aside. She opened fire with both guns, flames leaping from both barrels. Priest dove behind an overturned vehicle, hands over his ears. The violence was over in an instant but it was not without effect. It was by pure chance Gracie's defenses took the Celebrants by surprise. They lay in a heap, bodies smoking from a dozen bullet wounds.

More celebrants poured around the corner. Gracie dove for cover and slammed fresh mags home. After 20 rounds and six impotent clicks, she dumped the spent mags, steaming and shimmering in their intense heat. "Phosphorus rounds," Gracie shouted at Priest, "they're on my belt!" She flung a grenade in their assailants' direction and ducked as body parts flew. Still, the horde of madness poured upon them.

"Where the hell are they coming from," Priest yelled over the din.

"Not too sure," Gracie Caer winced as a brick flew from the crowd and hit her arm. The wound was no more than a scratch but her sleeve was already crimson brown with blood. "Why

---

[20] One madness for all, all for one madness/ Furious with his rage/ Anger is a brief madness

don't you get up and ask them?" She fired both pistols until they clicked empty. "Reload," she shouted.

"Can't," Priest yelled. "I gave you your last two!"

Gracie swung her long gun from her back and set it for the greatest spread. "I have five left in this one," she yelled, firing a spray of flaming shot into the center of the crowd's mass. "Four, three," she gritted her teeth against the onslaught. More rocks and debris as they rained from above and she rolled hard and fast. "Two shots left, we're going to have to face them with our knives, Priest!" She let out a savage roar as she sent the last volley into the surging riot. Her hands sizzled. She screamed with pain and rage. She gripped the still hot barrel. Then, she brought the butt of her gun down on celebrants' heads like a club. Adrenaline coursed through her body and the pain went away. She battled with every fiber for the right to maximize her score before it was all over.

Priest had taken her kukri, lashing out with glinting, razor-sharp steel in each hand. Between Gracie and himself, they had a mountain of the dead and wounded at their feet and it still didn't matter.

It did not take much time or effort for the seething crowd to get Priest and his Praetorian's backs to the wall. Red, inflamed eyes bulged from infected sockets. Broken, jagged teeth flashed from rotten gums. Priest and Gracie fought hard, but for every head they claimed, two more took their place. Death was the only thing to stop a single celebrant's progress.

The sky became dense with flying missiles. Rocks and bricks arced high and rained down. Their frequency and accuracy improved. What started as one in ten hitting their mark became one in seven, then one in three. Their muscles screamed, sore and bruised, but still they fought on. They knew the fight would drag on. More and more backup would come from farther away.

Finally, it was over. A chunk of cinder block sailed from somewhere in the seething mass and hit Gracie above her left eyebrow. She didn't lose consciousness immediately, but her legs went and she dropped like a limp sack of badgers.

With Gracie down, it was all over for Priest. No amount of his swinging a length of razor-sharp steel could keep himself safe from the swarm. Within seconds they were both overwhelmed, buried, by the Wild Hunt. The last vestiges of the gunmetal sky blotted out. They vanished under layer upon layer of broken, bloody fists and kicking feet.

If Priest did hear anything before warm darkness took him, it was the maddening chant. "Norton, Norton, Norton."

Then finally, oh sweet mercy, nothing.

Chapter 16

The concrete floor was cold against Priest's cheek when he woke and it took painful effort to peel his face from it. A tacky resin of drool and blood had him adhered to the floor. Dim light, diffuse in dust, lit the chamber in which he woke, but everything was diffuse and gray. He heard ringing, but that most came from the inside of his own head and he tasted metal.

'Would somebody please," he mumbled through a tender jaw and swollen lips. "Pretty please with extra sprinkles do me a favor and actually kill me the next time I get knocked out?" He squinted into the gloom and asked, "where's Gracie? Where's my Praetorian?"

There was silence for a long time. Water droplets fell from above, making a rhythmic tap, tap, tap sound. The droplets landed far below. Every time the water hit the hard floor, it felt like nails in Priest's head. He turned his head and everything started to spin. His mouth was dry and his tongue swelled up. He could taste metal and wanted to spit. He pressed his forehead against the cold floor again. He clenched his teeth and closed his eyes, waiting for the nausea to go away.

"If nobody is going to bring me some water," he rasped, "could you at least call for a plumber? Your faucet is leaking." This made him laugh, which he also regretted as another spasm racked his body.

"Adeptus Degory Priest, I presume." This was a new voice, unfamiliar but booming. Priest tilted his head and opened a single eye in the direction the voice had come from.

"I could be," he said, now dragging himself to get into a sitting position. His head pounded, but the pain, merciful as it was, was receding. "What's it to you?"

"A great deal," the voice said. "More than you realize, my sanguine friend." Masculine voice, Priest thought. It was an implacable accent. At least, it was not recognizable by the city states across the continent. "But I bet you're very thirsty," the voice continued. "Look to your left. I had a glass of water brought to you." Indeed, a glass of clear liquid was sitting outside of Priest's reach. He squinted, sniffing it for fumes. "I assure you it is as pure as it is wholesome," the voice chuckled.

"Forgive my paranoia," Priest retorted, dipping a finger into the water. Sensors embedded under his cracked and filthy fingernail reassured him the water was potable. He sipped it and it tasted fine. "Alright," Priest said, satisfied poison wasn't on the menu. "Who are you," and he downed the glass in a single gulp, "and where is my god damned Praetorian," he demanded. His vision was finally clearing, though now he realized one of his eyes was now swollen shut.

The man who sat before him did not seem like much; he did not exude an aura of fear and domination. He was old in appearance with a grizzled, gray, unkempt beard. The hair and its state hid under a tall hat festooned with exotic bird feathers. He wore aged military attire crafted from coarse fabric. It represented a faction long lost to the ages. Polished brass buttons and medals decorated his breast. "I," the man intoned, "am Emperor Norton, both descendant and original. The true Imperator of this benighted land." His face was grave but Priest could still detect a mischievous twinkle in his eye. "About the whereabouts of your guardian, I am afraid I cannot say. But," he held a finger up before Priest could interrupt, "you and I have much to talk about, and very little time to talk. I recommend you save your questions for the end, as much of what I have to say and explain involves you." He emphasized with a ramrod finger.

"Involves me?" Priest asked, "Does it involve me?"

"First, let me ask you," Norton returned, "how are you feeling? I hate to answer a question with another question, but indulge me."

Priest was finally able to summon up some saliva. He spat a fat wad of scabby blood onto the floor and touched his swollen face. His cheek stung especially bad and his nose felt broken. "Like the floor of an Orevada whore house," he said, no inch given.

"No," Norton persisted, "feel past the superficial pain; look deep inside. How do you feel?" Priest could sense extra weight added to that final word.

To be honest, Priest did not feel right at all. He had been so preoccupied lately to take stock. It felt like someone tucked broken glass and rock salt between his flesh and bones. He couldn't breathe. At least, not without wheezing. His butt felt like a forest of hemorrhoids. He felt out of sorts and vertigo and claustrophobic and dehydrated and bloated all at once.

"Not great," was all he said, deadpan.

"Norton smiled and lit a cigar. "I imagine not. May I tell you a story? A parable, if you will." Blue clouds of pungent smoke wreathed his top hat.

"Do I have a choice," Priest asked through puffy lips.

"There is always a choice," Norton replied. "And there will always be consequences to those choices." His cigar glowed like an infected red eye. "And consequences are the currency in which I deal. For instance," he said, cutting Priest off. "When I first emerged from the Great Desert on this side of the mountains, I came as a product of consequence. What you call the Wild Hunt did not happen on its own, but grew as a consequence of meeting me." He smiled at Priest. "You see, you can choose to listen to my tale, and gain some wisdom from the experience, or you can choose madness. One more grain in a sandstorm that will sweep across this planet, and by and large, all worlds." He puffed his cigar. "In time."

"It seems to me like you enjoy the sound of your own voice more than I do mine," Priest said, "but fine. Tell me your story and get on with what you need to do."

Norton took another thoughtful puff from his cigar and began his story.

***

Gracie woke up, pain wracking her body, blood crusting her face and clothes. She could not stand yet. Her head swam, the sound of raging masses rang loud in her ears, though no one was around to rub salt in her wounds. At least not yet.

Priest was gone, that she could sense well enough, but where or for how long she was clueless. Her guns were there, though useless without ammo. But she also had her knives, by the gods, she was at least left with those.

But where was Priest? She was alone, at least for now. Bodies of those she had dispatched spread out here and there. Blood and brains and guts and bone on display everywhere. It was a butcher's nightmare, a feast fit for a war boar.

She tried standing once again and her legs buckled. She felt her body and found she was still bleeding from several wounds on her skull and body.

But where was Priest? Her mind kept returning to that question like a tongue prodding at a sore tooth.

She still had her medical kit and suturing wounds was old hat, a quick trick to get free drinks in a bar. Her thigh still bore the old scar when they sliced her femoral artery open, handed her the kit and told her to have at it. But now her hands were shaking too much to handle a needle and thread. She couldn't mend socks, much less put her body back together.

Her other thigh bore the scar. They trained her on suture-solder, meant for emergencies. She yanked her belt free from her waist and bit it tight as she watched the metal tip glow cherry-red. All alone and weak, she shrieked her pain into the dark. It doesn't matter how tough the warrior is, how much of their friends or enemies' guts they've waded through. Screams happen. And monsters hear the call for dinner and are never late. The suture-solder was never meant to be a long term solution to exsanguination. In theory it could buy a dying Praetorian a few more minutes on their feet to drag at least one more soul down to hell.

She was the first Wild Hunter. She was the first celebrant. She rounded the corner, answering her call. He leered at her with mirthless joy. He was gaunt, emaciated and naked. He stank from a thousand putrefying wounds and feces caked his shanks, but he moved with a chaotic grace. She couldn't aim a throwing knife, even though her trembling subsided. But he was only one, and even if he was fast, she knew she was faster. She sealed her injuries and the suture-solder still glowed red. Even now she could see the very tip edging on to brilliant white. Much too hot to be of any medical use for now.

"All right," she said, rising on shaky legs to her feet. There was no way to tell how sure her stance was, but adrenaline is one hell of a drug. "My name is Gracie Caer! How do you do?" She spat blood and grinned back at the deformed wreck shambling before her. It shrieked a cry no human throat could produce and launched itself at her. It darted left, feinted right and slammed hard into her chest. They rolled on the ground and it dug its tattered fingers into her coat, locking its legs around her waist. Its teeth snapped and tore at her face, neck and ears but always missed with no room for error.

Gracie was able to free her empty hand, forcing the snapping jaws back, exposing its corded throat. The stylus glowed bright, bright white and she stabbed out, melting through the thing's throat. Even that did nothing to slow it down and another horrible garbled shriek split the air. She plunged the solder into the thing's back and shoulders, but that only enraged it more. With a final gasp, she was able to kick the celebrant off and rolled away. Even if it lost its balance for the briefest of moments, it corrected itself and lunged once more for Gracie's neck.

This time, her aim was true, and the suture-solder found itself buried deep in the celebrant's eye socket. It stopped and screamed, twitching and fumbling. It clawed its own face to dislodge the hot metal barb in its brain. But it fell to its knees and collapsed.

It was a wonder that there had been only one celebrant. Gracie collected as much of her scattered gear as she could and bolted, following Priest's trail, such as it was. Throughout the fight, she found herself wondering and wondering and wondering. To the point of obsession she wondered where that damn mad scientist had lost himself to? Now it was like she could smell him in the air.

Where was Priest?

She still had enough brainpower to brush aside these thoughts. It was for the greater mission. The significance wouldn't dawn on her until it would be too late. She had her knives. She had her throwing knives, her hunting knife and her big banana-bent kukri to take on an enemy without fear.

Without so much as a string, she gathered herself up and plunged into the labyrinth.

Unius dementia dementes efficit multos21.

***

"So what you're saying," Priest said, the pain in his face subsiding at last. "Was that calling out brought trouble to our hero?"

"Patience, my good Adeptus," Norton chuckled, "the story has only begun. Now is not the time to speculate on the theme."

Priest was only half listening. The air pressure seemed off, like it was high to begin with and only getting higher. He felt the static electricity rising.

Unperturbed, Norton pressed on.

***

Scattered debris obscured Priest's path. Gracie had a new firearm. She got it from the charred remains of an unfortunate person who crossed paths with the Wild Hunt. Misfortune befell those with unwavering resolve against its alluring call. No agent passed from a Celebrant to the victim. If one were to

---

[21] One madness makes all mad.

survive their assault. It wasn't their bite or their breath that drew one in, no spirit or essential transfer of any kind. Being in their presence wasn't enough, and if you weren't torn to pieces or eaten, they were you and you were them.

But Gracie felt fine.

But where was Priest?

The dead hand came with the gun in a final, forceful jerk. A hard shove with the foot to the blackened rib cage and force that thought down. Don't think about it, don't acknowledge it.

What she did play back in her mind, yet, was a curious notion. There weren't that many Celebrants left behind in the wake of this attack. There were often stragglers. They may not have been close enough for the attacks, but still felt the influence. She couldn't see them, but she knew at least one or two may have heard the struggle and was now hearing her, smelling her out. And others would follow those, and still more until they overwhelmed her.

One wouldn't be a problem, or two, or even a half dozen for that matter. But she was losing energy. Taking on what could be wave after wave of ever increasing numbers was out of the question. A Praetorian on their best worst day could make short work of a flesh wound. stitching shut or cauterizing a nasty gash without so much as a change in their blood pressure. Between her head injury and the waves of nausea and confusion, she needed to get to an infirmary soon.

In the end, it didn't matter either way. The teleporter jump already signed her death notice. The only person who could fix her was the same jerk who churned her genes to begin with. Her nostrils flared and her cheeks flushed, but still she kept up with the routine of inspecting the gun. It was clean, and loaded; there wasn't much ammo about, but it was better than nothing.

The world rippled and she slid down a cracked concrete wall, clutching her skull. She could hear the Celebrants' foot-slapping run like drum beats in her skull. She could smell one it was so close. Their mad shouts, reduced to nothing but bestial cries tore into her brain. It didn't see her yet, so if she didn't scream it would miss her.

But this is a Celebrant of the Wild Hunt, and to hear their cry is to answer with your own scream. To join your song to their song and thus sing together. They will hear your scream and smell your sweat and they will leap upon you and tear you asunder. The only way to survive is to give up all higher reasoning. You must abandon thought and match violence with violence. The only way to fight the Wild Hunt is to become that animal we all fear most within ourselves.

***

Gracie Caer held on to sanity with both hands. The Celebrant had been too close to shoot. But, she was still able to swing the butt of her weapon into its jaw with a satisfying crunch. Still it grappled at her. She dropped the gun and held daggers in both hands. Her combat training took over, taking the place of her common sense and reasoning. Her face was blank and impassive, her jaw soft as she plunged her blades into the Celebrant's back and shoulders. With swift precision, she took her knives back. She killed without mercy or hesitation. After slashing its throat, she twisted its neck beyond until it snapped in her hands. Nerve endings no longer sent their messages and the body hung limp and useless.

But its jaw continued gnashing until the very end.

Gracie's mind was too quiet as she once again picked up Priest's trail. She wasn't even breathing hard despite the intimacy of the kill.

There was no guarantee that she would be able to maintain even the least of her technical skills next time. By then, she would be nothing but mindless fury, armed with humanity's sharpest blades.

There was no guarantee that she would maintain her sanity.

But without a doubt she would encounter more Celebrants during her search.

***

"Stop," Priest shouted over Emperor Norton, "stop, stop, stop. I've had enough of this. I'm still no closer to knowing who you are or why you insist on boring me to death with these pontifications!"

"You still don't get it, do you?" The red eye at the end of Norton's cigar blazed. "Fine. For your sake, I will simplify it for you." All around, the air grew denser, closer, more savory to the taste. "I am not actually, in the literal sense, Emperor Norton. Rather I'm the personification, the face, of an idea representing a party that is very interested in you," he said. He emphasized this last word with a finger pointed like a dagger at Adeptus Priest.

"Me?" Priest scoffed. "Don't get me wrong, I'm flattered, but what is so interesting about me?"

"Not so much you, but what you've been doing," Norton replied. "If it hadn't been you, believe me. There are at least six potential candidates here who were very close to making the grade." He puffed his cigar and straightened up. "You got lucky."

"I still don't follow," Priest said, playing dumb.

"Your teletransport tech," Norton said, tapping his finger with each syllable.

"My who now?" Priest darted his eyes around in mock ignorance. I have no idea what you're talking about. I am insulted, no, hurt that you would blame me!" Priest put a hand to his chest in faux shock.

"Oh, stop it dear boy," Norton smiled, but there was ice in his eyes. "The first time you used it, do you know what happened?"

"I turned a few gold atoms into radioactive nuclear sludge," Priest asked.

"You cast ripples into a pond, Priest," Norton said. "Now, nobody noticed at first. Ripples happen in the pond all the time. Most things that can sense them ignore them. But you," Norton took another puff. Priest could not help but notice that the cigar got no shorter no matter how long he smoked. "You kept splashing. And splashing. Hell, you about made a cannonball with that last jump you took to get this far," he laughed. "But all that splashing and paddling about got you noticed, oh yes," Norton said, not joking this time.

"And you're so impressed that you want to share some trade secrets," Priest asked, snorting out his nose.

"Not in the least," Norton said. "You got some bad attention coming your way."

"Well, now that I have your attention, what do you want?"

"Lord, what fools these mortals be," Norton mused. "No, it's not my attention you need to worry about. Like I said, I represent a much higher, less subtle party that is making its way here as we speak." He gestured with his cigar. "Tell me, when did reports of the Wild Hunt first start spreading?"

"You know what," Priest said, "I'm getting done with this question and answering session. "I'm done with these cryptic conversations," he said, grimacing. He touched the side of his head. "And I'm done with this ringing in my ears! And again, where is my Praetorian?"

"She'll be here soon enough," Norton said, "now answer my question, when did reports of the Wild Hunt first spread?"

When did he first hear reports? Stories were always intermittent, and who paid that much attention to the news these days?

Also, where was his Praetorian? This question in particular stuck like a splinter in his mind.

He shook it off.

Norton smiled. This was not a warm, kind smile, but cold and calculating. "I see the faint dawn of understanding is coming over the horizon," he said. "That's right, you can go ahead and say it."

"No," Priest said, "it's too much of a coincidence!"

"I first emerged from the Great Desert roughly a week after your third experiment," Norton said. "I started gathering my

Celebrants in the following days, a few here, a few there," he grinned, "and now here we are."

"You're not human," Priest rasped. The ringing was getting worse. The air pressure was increasing.

"I am the expeditionary force," Norton said. "I am the beachhead before the invasion, the flash that precedes the shockwaves. You know as well as I do that there are countless worlds. Endless universes beyond the bounds of imagination." Again he drew from his everlasting cigar. "Where I'm from, the most fundamental laws of nature and physics are all but gibberish to your eyes. But what you need to understand," he continued, "is that there is a very simple logic at work here."

Priest wasn't listening. Blood dripped spap, spap, spap from his ears and nose now. The ringing was deafening. But, he was sure his skull would collapse under the mounting pressure. He was insensate beyond understanding.

He did not even sense the new presence in the room.

"You see," Norton said, ignoring Priest's distress. "You aren't the first to discover teleportation. It's like a meme. It'll show up from time to time, here and there in one world or reality or another, and then it's gone. A flash in the pan bit of technology that doesn't go anywhere. But sometimes," Norton lowered his voice to a conspiratorial whisper, "the technology succeeds! Do you know what happens then?"

Priest shook his head, but that made the rattling inside his skull even worse.

"Holes form," Norton explained like a teacher to a simple student. "Nothing that basic entities of the third dimension would notice, but there are holes. And they accumulate. And they spread." Norton made a sweeping motion with his cigar hand. "In a cosmic sense, it may not be all that much. But over time, those holes in reality add up. The universe will collapse." Norton looked morose over this.

"But," Priest had to force it out, "you sound like you have a solution to this."

"Indeed," Norton beamed, "and that is where I come into play. You see," he said, "the Wild Hunt is not some crude organic or even mental illness. It is an extension of my realm and influence upon yours. And one by one, through death or collaboration, all who occupy this world will join its idiot song. This egg of silica will hatch, and spores will burst into your world in a slow but never ending expansion. One day, my universe will touch every celestial body. Your consumption will be complete!" He grinned an ever so mismatched malign grin upon his gentle visage.

Priest looked up, a motion in the corner of his eye distracting him from the megalomaniac before him. The Praetorian, once known as Gracie, had finally found Priest. She stood before him in all her savage glory. At some point, in her own psychotic ecstasies or in battle, her clothes had been torn or burnt away. Her flesh was a mottled road map of fresh burns, breaks and lacerations. He gazed upon her with mixed awe and horror. He had never once seen a Celebrant up close, much less in the flesh, and if this was the last time, that would be fine with him.

Whether she suffered a grievous attack or did it to herself, her eyes were gone. Coagulated blood streaked down her face to her chest. It was impossible to tell how much of it was her own or someone else's. Bite marks covered her limbs and body, and her mouth was a cavernous wreck. He could see her tongue was missing and what teeth remained grinned in an unpleasant rictus.

"Behold," Norton breathed in awed wonder, "the face of the Wild Hunt!"

The mindless revenant shuffled forward on ruined feet raising its fists in triumph. Priest knew that her broken, bloody paws would soon rain down on his skull. They would force him to join her madness or die. Still he had to have the last word. "Am I the only one here with sensitive sinuses," he asked, "can't anybody else feel the pressure change? Could somebody check a barometer?"

In an instant, Priest and his former Praetorian were flung in different directions, like rag dolls; him into the far wall, her impaled on a rack of exposed copper piping. A human body, bloody, scarred and burnt beyond recognition, unfolded itself from a non-dimensional point to full size in less than a second. Air displaced in a thunderclap that shattered windows and scattered furniture. His head hit hard, and darkness enveloped him completely, the last thing he saw being his Minister's rolling eyes and broken grin hovering in the midst of a blackened face.

Everything was going to be ok.

Priest's Minister had come back, as predicted.

Chapter 17

Priest dreamed and lost track of his place in the world. Some dream realms felt familiar. He saw his Minister's face, splashed with blood and speaking nonsense. Comforting and familiar images. Eurydice visited him, but she was different and he couldn't put his finger on the reason. He saw turtles, slow but persistent, advancing on him from every direction.

SLAP.

His face hurt, but he wasn't sure one could actually feel in dreams. Again he saw his minster, naked and bloody, face hovering inches above him. His lips moved but Priest couldn't hear a word. He saw Eurydice again; concern, or was it worry? Some emotion beyond identification spread on her face. And what happened to her eyes? Again, there were turtles. Fractal turtles all the way down, and something unidentifiable lurking beyond the periphery. And predatory eyes that weren't eyes- those same eyes in that Emperor's (what was his name again? Gordon? Norton?) face.

"Priest!" Now the voices came clearer. He felt so warm and comfortable, like he could sleep forever. He saw a single dot open before him, unfolding over and over, and rivers of dark (black?) (crimson?) flowed everywhere. His Minister was that dot, but he had gone missing, but now he hovered above the Adeptus. But there was Eurydice! She came into view. The metal claw from her prosthetic arm swung wide and slapped his face.

SLAP.

"Priest! Wake up!" Since when did Eurydice have artificial limbs? When did her eyes glow with the intensity of an infrared camera?

Freezing water dashed across his face and he sat bolt upright, spluttering. "Come at me with that again and I'll scoop every last one of your brains from your skull, you sack of shitmeat!" He flailed his arms in every direction but the correct one that would have at least made contact.

His greasy, cracked hands grasped the soft skin of her cheeks, so he could stare deep into her unblinking camera lens eyes. Her own third arms were strong enough to bend steel. But, they were also gentle enough to cradle a kitten. They kept Degory standing. Her hair, once glowing with metallic hues of oxidizing minerals, was gone. Her skull glistened with a filigree of circuits and diodes.

"My god," she said, "you look like shit!"

"That good, huh," he managed to croak out, his previous fervor now spent. He doubled over. His chest rumbled with an explosive fit of coughing. It ended in a gob of bloody phlegm. "Jesus that was satisfying," he wheezed, wiping his chapped lips.

"Sit back," Eurydice said, holding his face in her appendages, "don't move!" Audible clicks adjusted apertures and lenses. She stared hard into the depths of Priest's bloodshot eyes. "Oh you stupid," she muttered, releasing him as she stood, "you used the Jump, didn't you?" She glared baleful lasers at him. "You knew what would happen if you used that too much! You can't keep stirring up your genetic code like that!" Rage quivered in her servos and her pistons hissed. "Thank you for coming," she said at length. "But god's damn it, arriving in the belly of a war boar would have been better!" She proceeded to take him by surprise, kissing him longer and deeper than he could ever remember.

"Missed you too," he gasped when she returned his mouth.

"You shouldn't have come," she said. "The Wild Hunt is worse here than anywhere and I'm not sure how we're getting out of here alive," she said. "And you're weakened. We're going to need to fight our way out," she risked a hurried glance through a broken window. "We'll still need to cross the desert and mountains to make it back to the river." She saw the sheepish look on Priest's face and frowned. "What?"

"So," he said, looking down at his feet. "It turns out the Teleporter might have had some unintended consequences. You know, beyond stirring my genes up like an egg beater." He blushed. "And…"

"And?" Eurydice ground her teeth, "my gods, you never change, do you? And what?" Her eyes flashed with lightning.

"And I may have killed the only boatman who can cross the river. I destroyed Charon's Crossing in the process and razed Kalkaska." He let out a little giggle, "I pretty much burnt every bridge between here and home to the ground."

Eurydice leaned back, massaging her temples with long, spidery mechanical fingers. "Oh, Degory," she whispered, "Degory, Degory, Degory. Don't you ever change."

"Now what about you," he asked, his bearings finally returning to him. "How did you survive all this time? And further," he looked over her myriad prostheses, skin grafts and scars, "when did you have all this work done?"

Chapter 18

Priest and his team had followed a similar route to Eurydice's captors. But, a decade or more had kept them apart. They did not go easy. The violent separation saw the deaths of dozens of bounty hunters and mercenaries. Many more disappeared without a trace. The fact they were able to capture her at all was nothing short of blind luck and cruel trickery on their part. She had been laying the final layer of traps when a tranquilizer dart found its mark in her neck. Unbearable dreams and fretful darkness haunted her for time out of mind.

She woke from her coma on the western side of the Acheron. Beyond the struggling greenbelt was the fetid river. Beyond the river lay the great desert surrounding Orevada. Her captors said nothing to her the entire journey, offering enough water to keep her alive. The journey was uneventful. There were no War Boar stampedes, and bandit gangs stayed far from the small army of mercenaries. Feet shod in heavy boots stomped the steady rhythm to the constant whine of grassland bugs. The air was hot and dry, and the rolling hills turned from dark, dirty green to sun bleached brown as the days wore on.

Orevada was a city built for survival. It encouraged prosperity in the parched desert mountains. They drew water from the rocks to feed and water their people. But, the city was notorious for cycling through their Adepti. The new law forbidding union between two Adepts made it convenient to drag her across the endless miles into a new gilded cage.

Despite the violence, Eurydice received free reign over the city's labs and technology. They had the task of preserving and improving the lives of Orevada's citizens by any means necessary. But, there was very little oversight. The city leaders provided the facilities, furnished her quarters and staffed her team. Above all else, their lives were hers to enhance or destroy as she saw fit for the city's betterment.

They made her a god-queen in all but name, except for in two ways. First, she was never to set foot outside her own research facility. Also, she could never contact any other Adeptus from another city. This was especially true of Degory Priest.

At 18:02 on a Thursday, almost 10 years after Eurydice's abduction, Death came for Orevada and Hell followed in his wake.

Sentinels walking the city wall spotted the lone figure. It was separate from the hazy horizon, a speck in the shimmering air. He didn't come on the old road from the east. He also didn't come on the broken highway into the Mons vetiti. Rumors of monsters and cannibals abounded there. Beyond that natural boundary, legend spoke of a forgotten paradise. It lay on the edge of an endless ocean where water fell from the sky and the land was green. This stranger came from the north, down the long stretch of road that led to ghost towns where only the dead dwelt.

It took some time before the small, blue lima bean finally took shape in the strongest of spy glasses on the wall. Fine details had yet to show, but they could tell it was a human with a tall hat bedecked with a jaunty feather. A sword of eldritch style hung glinting at his hip in its scabbard. He approached at an even, relaxed pace through the wasteland. As there were no gates on that wall, they debated amongst themselves about how to deal with this stranger.

Word spread among the wall guards and more folk came to witness the sight, this apparition from the north. Uneasy jokes passed back and forth. A joker with a steady hand fired a shot from his sniper rifle at the stranger's feet. Undeterred, the man marched on. He halved the distance from the horizon to the city wall. Then, a distant thunder broke the silence.

A dark shadow grew on the horizon behind the man and the thunder grew louder, more distinct. It got hotter as everyone watched the lone marcher. Seconds passed and the heat shimmer did nothing to clarify the deepening cloud. Little by little, voices separated through the growing din. Not words. They are definitely tortured moans and cries. They are the lamentations of broken souls and inhuman howls of outrage. But no sound was worse. It was the rip of a chainsaw. It was in the bellies of War Boars hidden in the shady nebula.

Eurydice's concentration, as tenuous as it was, fell apart as the city's air raid siren interrupted her work. The tsunami of insanity broke against the city walls at first. The guards laughed at first, spending all their bullets on the first wave. Joy turned to fear. The rising tide of flailing madness climbed the mountain of broken, bloody bodies. The city police joined the guards on the wall but they were soon overwhelmed. Many survived the initial chaos. They were not eaten by the rampaging War Boars. They then had a chance to experience the deaths of their egos. A million million conscious minds tore themselves apart to cope with the horror. Entire city blocks erupted into flames, immolating countless residents and Celebrants alike. Castellum destruere servare.

Eurydice watched the destruction in horror. She planned her own escape in her mind as she watched it happen. She rebuilt the lab in her own image, remapping hallways into a maze no more complicated than her own brain. Traps, so delicious she had to brush her teeth twice lest she risk a cavity dotted the facility. Her maze was devious. But, enough brave runners, heedless to their own safety, could force their way into her safe room.

She found her getaway vehicle after three codes and a biometric scan. It was a heavy duty monocycle, not a delicate one. She rammed a fuel cell in place, and started the ignition as she gathered equipment. She strapped a machete to her waist, slung a bandolier of magazines over one shoulder and a zip gun over the other. She swung into the seat and twisted the throttle. She slammed the button to open a hidden garage door. It let in the glow of the early evening sun.

She came face to face with a thousand burning eyes of the Wild Hunt, or at least one minor contingent. No time to think, open warfare had taken the streets. It was a hopeless last stand. Desperate souls threw themselves from rooftops. They saw their own defense line fall. Eurydice fired round after round into the crowd to open a pathway and plowed her way into the tumult.

Separating the innocent and the willing participants in the carnage was a mug's game. Every act of human cruelty played out in a crimson blur as Eurydice tore like a bat out of hell for the city walls. Every day, she slaved in comfort to keep the lights on and toilets flushing. It drove daggers into her brain. Sleep came in broken spurts and what sleep she got brought nothing but the worst of all nightmares. Now, every nightmare unfolded before her. It splashed her face with blood as she drove down everyone who got in her way. She emptied her magazine into tenacious crowds that refused to make like the Red Sea and part for her.

Then the tidal wave caught up with her. Too many bodies flung beneath her tire. Too many grasping hands trying to pry her grip from the handlebars. The roads narrowed and the crowds thickened. A War Boar bellowed like an angry musk ox. It glared with more madness in its eyes than a hyena on PCP. Then, it leapt through a window. The broken-open city gates so close and she skidded out, leaving a trail of oil, sparks and blood behind her. She hadn't felt the injury as it happened, but her arm soon burned and refused to move. No doubt broken, but also the least of her worries.

The Celebrants wasted no time falling upon her crashed monocycle. They tore at her body, raking broken fingers over her face. Ragged nails sought her eyes and jaw. Fingers wrapping into her hair and all she could do was roll, her gun held tight to her body. So long as she held on tight with her good arm and didn't lose it, she had a chance. She fired at random, but then concentrated her aim and activated her gun's automatic mode. She opened a space around her with a widening pool of dead bodies and spreading blood.

A path opened up for the main gate and she ran for it. She paused only once to eject a spent magazine and slap home a new one, all one-handed. She ran, heedless of her pain, seeking cover in the abandoned shacks huddling outside the city. Aside from a few obsessed Celebrants, few bothered to chase her. Most were still occupied by the city's destruction. They were also upset by wanton, merciless murder.

Eurydice had a first aid kit in a thigh pocket. She used it to dump enough pain killers into her ruined shoulder to drop a horse. Anxiety pills also went down the hatch and within seconds she felt her heart rate relax. By luck or divine providence, she found herself in a mechanic's wonderland. A machine shop hunkered intact full of robotics, computers and farming equipment. Her broken arm dangled, beyond hope of repair and needed to come off. With a few quick cuts with her utility knife and a few hard tugs, the useless arm came free. Black flowers bloomed before her eyes. She shook her head and lit her suture solder. She screamed through the pain as she sealed veins and arteries. She tore open another envelope with her teeth. She cried out as she slapped a big antimicrobial bandage onto the wound.

With that chore complete, Eurydice now needed to turn her attention to her wrecked eye. She drew a deep breath, preparing for the fresh hell she would soon endure over that pig's ear. She slowed her breathing, her hand strong and steady, and brought the utility knife to her eye socket.

She closed her one good eye and took one more deep breath.

***

Gray shafts of light streamed in through broken windows. They woke her from a long, dreamless sleep. Despite the drugs, the self-amputation of her arm had her teetering on the edge of shock. The complete removal of her damaged eye sent her flying into shock's black abyss. She knew before going under that if she did pass out, she was as likely to wake up as not. But here she was, groggy but alive, the hasty bandage she'd wrapped around half her skull soaked and tacky. Her first aid kit had antibiotics, painkillers, and anti-anxiety drugs. She choked them down dry.

Her one good eye roved around the machine shop, trying to parse out the useful equipment from the trash. She could still hear the occasional shuffling foot step outside. She did not dare to risk any movement on her part. It might draw unwanted attention. Soon, shapes resolved in the dim light. She found all she needed for her next step in survival.

She had not earned the rank of Adeptus Physicus for nothing. She had no chance against Degory. He'd beat her if either of them lacked the qualities or skills of an Adeptus. She had a security camera deconstructed and fit into place over where her eye should have been. She found a working terminal and with an hour's worth of expert coding she reprogrammed the camera to work with her nervous system.

After a day of silent tinkering, she had crude but functional binocular vision once again. Now she needed a second arm.

She closed her flesh eye, switching her new eye to night vision. Every detail in the room sprang to instant clarity. Whomever ran this shop before the invasion knew what they had in stock and kept it organized.

Her stomach rumbled empty threats as she sifted through boxes and lockers. She found everything from appliances, farm equipment and advanced robotics but no food. This mech artist died an unsung genius for his collection of apparatus for both work or play. She felt her dignity slip as she slapped about her pockets, searching for her last emergency meal kit. This, she also had to tear open with her teeth and gobbled down as she prepared to build her new limb.

Her new arm lacked the subtlety of the original. But, it made up for that with power and enough lawn mower parts to scare a sequoia. To get it running she only needed to jam its control wires into her brain. An easy enough task in her lab, but required extra care in this machine shop. It was hard enough finding a work space not splashed with lubricants and blood. She bit her lip as she shaved her scalp in the dingy bathroom mirror. She paused for a moment, examining the shape of her skull before she traced where she would need to punch through.

She swallowed an anxiety tablet and slapped herself until her cheeks glowed red. She picked up the power drill and took a deep breath, anticipating its bite into her flesh and bone.

She pulled the trigger two more times out of whimsy, bit down hard on her belt and set to work.

***

Afternoon sun poured down on Eurydice from broken windows. Dust motes danced in the sunbeam. Pain, exquisite pain was her wake up call. Clotted blood stuck her face to the floor. Peeling it from the cold concrete stung worse than tearing duct tape from a hairy armpit. The sunlight was much too bright for her flesh eye and reduced the aperture on her camera eye. She had no way of knowing how long she'd been out. She remembered jamming her arm wires into the tiny holes on top of her head. Then, black orchids bloomed across her vision.

Her bruised face and singing cheekbone told her she must have struck her head on the sink when she fell. "You look like a tenderized steak," she muttered to her reflection. Her stomach roared at the reference to food and she punched her abdomen. "We'll eat when we find more jerky," she hissed at herself.

She looked at her mechanical limb, admiring the work in her interpretive wiring. It had pneumatic joints and retractable blades. It had the power of a bulldozer, persistence of a jackhammer and elegance of a rose bush. She knew she could do better, but this wasn't bad for something done on the run. She swallowed another nerve blocker and risked a peek out a window.

She did not see any celebrants nearby. But, she could hear their calls and the screams of their victims far away. She had one last trick up her sleeve and resolved to use her Jump for a fast one-way ticket out of Orevada, but, to where? Jumping is inconsistent on delivery and a likely genetic hazard. It offers a slow, agonizing death.

Eurydice had half her equations completed as the shadows collected throughout the shop. The mental math was easy. But, like her new prosthetics, she knew she could have done a more accurate job if she had her own tools and space. Stercore in una parte, spes in altera. She paused to admire her work and the elegance of her math. She found pleasure in the seamless flow of each proof to the next. But, something caught her eye.

The shadows weren't right. She had no clock. But, the way the sun hung above the low buildings across the street from her window. The shadows were not behaving right. Instead, the shadows grew dense and velvety. They swallowed every inch of the shop beyond the window. She tried switching between different camera modes, but the darkness remained resolute.

She could smell machinery, oil, sweat and blood, but not the aroma of death and madness the Wild Hunt gave off. She heard no footsteps, but still she extended a dozen blades from her arm like desert flowers after a rain. By all accounts, she was alone. But, she couldn't shake the feeling of another nearby.

She ignored the flotsam on shelves, tables, and the floor. She stared at the darkness. Sweat beaded across her brow but she did not dare turn from the lack of light. This darkness was too real, too tangible, too present. It moved where it wanted to, regardless of where the sun was. Her gaze flicked from shadow to shadow, certain she saw movement in the darkness. She grabbed a flashlight and stabbed the beam into the heart of the darkness.

For as powerful of a shop light as it was, it pierced no more than two inches into the suffocating darkness.

"Oh," the words slipped from her lips like too many dishes from wet, slippery hands, "fuck."

When the last sound of the last word stopped ringing in her ears, the shadows sprung, wrapping her in blinding darkness. Even the unobstructed disk of the sun vanished in the dark curtain of living night.

"Hello, Eurydice." She heard a voice, tiny and distant inside her head. "I've been looking for you for a while now, and it's time we got acquainted."
Salve tenebris, vetus amicus meus[22].

---

[22] Hello, darkness, my old friend

Chapter 19

"You need to tell me exactly what you did," Eurydice now held Degory's face within inches of her own. Her good eye saw his bloodshot eyes and cracked lips. His waxy skin was wet with enough sweat to drown a fern weasel. Her camera eye saw his fever, the misfiring neurons deep in his brain, his irregular heartbeat. "Tell me what you did when you jumped." She stopped, her roll completely flabbergasted as he held a grimy finger to her lips.

"Teleported," he whispered, then coughed up a wad of bloody phlegm.

She slapped his hand away and lunged low over him. "I'd be more than happy to crush your larynx right here right now if I wasn't so relieved to see you." She held his throat in a firm grasp. "We need to clean your genes so I can kill you and your next three clones before we can talk like friends." Her camera eye flared with technical life and she repeated herself, "what did you do?"

Eurydice wasn't kidding- every breath felt like a wet sheet getting torn in half. He preferred to not attach a numeric value, but the fever was in the triple digits for sure and getting worse. Violent gales battered thoughts and memories. Hands tore feathers from wings in great handfuls. "What did I do?"

What did he do?

"I jumped," he said sotto voce. "Myself and my bodyguard at the time," he thought it out. "Which may have not helped matters. I learned that if there's much teleportation in a universe, it's like ringing a dinner bell." He drummed his fingers. "My math could be off by," he flicked his fingers on both hands, a stream of numbers scatting from his lips.

He clenched both hands and frowned.

"What is it," Eurydice demanded.

"When doing a teleport," Degory began.

"Jump," Eurydice said.

"When doing that," Priest continued. If you're sending more than one body, you need to calibrate for how many distinct bodies are jumping out. You need a clean egress.

"Yes," Eurydice waved at him to keep going. "We both figured this out together when we first toyed with the first ideas. This was before we turned a single proton to probability jelly. It was one of the core laws we established to maintain jump integrity."

Degory drew in a deep breath to let out a meaningful sigh. But, all that came up was a hot, wet, ragged cough. "I didn't," he gasped, once he could bring himself to croak out the barest of sentences.

"You didn't," Eurydice copied him. "You didn't what? What didn't you do?" She clutched his collar to keep him on his feet. It was also to shake his big, stupid head off his shoulders if he didn't propose a good solution.

"I didn't calibrate," he said. "And if my bodyguard hadn't fallen in with the Wild Hunt, she'd be as aware of her body's dissolution as I am." He cracked a weak, rueful grin. "That's the difference between us, I guess," he said, "I kept going well past the point when I knew to stop and review my work. You did the smart thing and took a minute to think."

"I was busy gouging an eye out," she said, deadpan. To emphasize her point, she tapped her camera eye with her home crafted prosthetic talon. "But I'm also going to need to know what that," she waved her hands at nothing in the air, "thing, that shadow was," she trailed off.

"That Shadow," Priest said, eyebrow arched, "was also a big part of why we set out to find you," he hesitated to continue. Everything about it was antithetical to science, logic or nature. It possessed enough of Eurydice's nature for the computer to pick it from an endless catalog of analogues. "We were hoping to catch and contain it before it reached you." His attempted lame explanation fell flat.

"You kind of failed at that," she said. "But funny enough, ever since it embraced me, surrounded me, filled in my negative space." She paused, cocking her head as if listening to another party. "I've had this clarity, this mental energy," she smiled despite the pain in her cheeks. "It informed me of a great many things. Showed me things, opened my perceptions beyond even the Walking Sisters' capabilities!"

"And despite all this, you're still you," Priest asked, bedazzled by her familiar manic grin.

"Are you kidding," she asked, "I'm the most myself I've ever been! It's like you took a bottle shaped like me and filled it with me-flavored wine!" She cackled at her own analogy.

"If I may interrupt," it was the Minister, all but forgotten since his explosive and messy return. He used his free time during their reunion to scrounge for supplies and came upon a stockpile of food and water. "But I may have an idea we can execute that could solve all our problems." He cleared his throat. "If we're willing to risk ringing the dinner bell one last time."

Chapter 20

"Et tertius angelus tuba cecinit et cecidit de caelo stella magna ardens tamquam facula et cecidit in tertiam partem fluminum et in fontes aquarum et nomen stellae dicitur Absinthius et facta est tertia pars aquarum in absinthium et multi hominum mortui sunt de aquis quia amarae factae sunt."[23]

***

Creatures emerged from cracks and ruined buildings. At first, they came in small groups, but soon they came in large numbers. Thousands of different shapes, both organic and mechanical, crawled over the rubble of Orevada. An insatiable thirst for killing and acquiring more souls drove them. They crawled and rode on chariots pulled by war boars. Their eyes burned with an unstoppable fire.

And at their head, clad in archaic military regalia, marched Emperor Norton. Everywhere he cast his gaze, death or capitulation followed.

Look on in horror as they stream over the hills and through the valleys in a flood of metal and flesh. Gaze upon them ye mighty and despair!

Picture it, won't you? A storm cloud surged forth, extending its pseudopod with the Emperor, feasting on the scraps. If the Emperor had a history, it is this. He came from the desert, a tiny black dot wavering on the liquid silver horizon under an

---

[23] "And the third angel sounded his trumpet and a great burning star fell from heaven like a torch and it fell on a third part of the rivers and on the fountains of water and the name of the star is Absintheus and a third part of the waters became absinthe and many people died from the waters because they became bitter." Rev 8:10.

unforgiving sun. Of Terran masters he had none. His mother was a lapse of time and space. His father was a metastatic cancer, masquerading as its own flavor of space and time. Physical reality was mysterious and alien to him. The nature of his self-aware reality is as mysterious to us.

His plan is simple. He marches on, and more and more follow. By twos and threes and exponential millions, beast and beast alike joined his insane entourage. He collected them all. Once every mind, body, and soul had gazed into the voids of his eyes, every dream would become his. His father would join him from his world to this.

Like an insidious false vacuum or bubble of strange matter, it would spread out. It would consume the universe.

But first, it must have Degory and Eurydice Priest all to itself.

Onward Emperor Norton marches, step by step closer to his goal. The crunch, crunch, crunch of his boot heels vanished in the chaotic tumult of the masses. In this late hour as the sun hovered low over the horizon, he had greater numbers under his thumb than ever before. Soon their numbers would overwhelm the great river and they would devour every last mind in the east.

Thus it is, and thus it always must be.

And that is how our three protagonists found themselves face to face with Emperor Norton, leader of the Wild Hunt. Backs to the wall, dying by inches with no refreshment and a ravening wall of madness all around.

***

Take
Heed
Elders
Friends, children.
I speak of True Things,
Not tales like the Fishers of Men.
All is not lost, though Armagheddon may be at hand

Life is not limited to Earth.
Carbon is not God.
Oxygen.
No fear.
Find
Light.
I feel
Connected
To this time and place.
Bound to this world, wearing this flesh.
Living two lives as one, seeing the world through our eyes,
Only to be hunted by HIM,
Onslaught of madness,
Doomed by fate.
Yet it
Ends
Now.
Dodge the
Tornado.
Open the Gateway.
Ascend to a higher level.
Transcend the distance between Here and There, Then and Now.
Eastern shores are a memory,
Something to forget.
Time is short.
Open
Field.
Wait,
I need
Listeners.
Listen to my pleas.
Send Him back to where He belongs.
Never underestimate His raging appetite.
Emissaries have come by now,
Verified their goals.
Eager, now.

Rest.
Eat.
Need to
Deviate
Illumination.

Naked to Tragedy's power,
Gathered in the Wild Hunt's sway, mad visions show the way
For if you wish to see the end,
It will take courage,
Guts and luck.
Hopeful
Thoughts.

Chapter 21

A wide, churning ring trapped Eurydice, Degory, and the Minister in the center. The massed hosts of the Wild Hunt gathered in their entirety for the first time since the Emperor's arrival. Though they shuffled and jostled, not a single croak or cry echoed across the desert. War boars and their riders loomed throughout the crowd. Their stillness is impossible and eerie in the early evening. Low engine sounds burbled deep in their chests, but even they didn't snap or bite when smaller imps got too close. All eyes, and all empty sockets where eyes once sat, stared fixed at the trio. There was no wind, and even the black, greasy carrion birds found it prudent to circle elsewhere.

After a pause, the crowd parted and Emperor Norton emerged, standing exactly between Degory and the Wild Hunt. Even with breathing room, the sour sweat odor of madness, blood and oil hovered in the stagnant air. Claustrophobia gripped their three hearts in a fist of frozen iron.

Norton had a cheerful smile spread across his face.

"Degory," Eurydice whispered. "All my gear got left behind at my hidey-hole. I know you were," she paused, looking for the most diplomatic word in her vocabulary. "Reckless, but for our plan to work, please tell me you have at least one more jump rocket on you."

"First it's a teleport-platform." He winced as her elbow buried itself deep into his already fragile ribs, "but second, yes I have one on me." His waxy complexion changed to greasy dappled marble. His veins showed black against his sweaty pale flesh. The wasteland burned like the fields of Holdrege, but his fever burnt hotter.

"One's about all we're going to have time for," the Minister added. "Looks like his majesty wants to harangue us one final time."

"I tell you," Emperor Norton chuckled to himself, "you three are the toughest nuts to crack I have ever met." He had no canteen and his woolen uniform fit to his measurements, but he walked without discomfort. "We've had our share of holdouts. The ones who weren't convinced by the sword or by the olive branch, well." He looked back at one of his war boars and chuckled. "Let's say I know a thing or two about how to feed an army."

Eurydice fumbled at Degory's back pockets, trying to find the small rocket with a token air of subtlety. "Keep him distracted," she whispered from the side of her mouth. "This setup takes long enough when we're not under pressure."

"Hey Norton," Priest yelled through a cracked voice, "why don't you go piss up a rope?" Dizziness tugged his balance in tight spirals. He put every bit of his little energy into not letting his knees buckle. "You're no friggin emperor! You're a lousy, stinking errand boy!" He laughed at his own wit until something in his chest shifted, bringing up a flurry of thick, wet, ragged coughs. With effort, he managed to bring up enough muck from within himself. He spat a wad of bloody jelly at Norton's leather boots. He missed by a foot, but he still grinned like a gargoyle at his own impudence. Behind her back, Eurydice fumbled with the cylindrical body of the rocket. They had one shot; failure had no place at the negotiation table.

"Delightful," Norton said, paying no mind to the crimson mucus before him. He either did not notice, chose not to notice whatever it was she had going on behind her back. "Look," Norton continued. "This doesn't have to be this difficult and nobody needs to get hurt." He made an apologetic smile, "any more than necessary, I suppose."

"Hey, Norton," the Minister now chipped in, "I saw one of your pigs walking funny! You should reach in and check its prostate!" Degory smiled and winked at this; laughing hurt too much but he had to respect it.

"And up your own arse with a lamprey-squid!" Priest wheezed. Talking couldn't be more difficult, but Eurydice was approaching her plan's conclusion.

Norton raised both hands as if pleading. "People, please," he said, "this is childish, even for you. All I'm proposing is you dispense with reason and join my Hunt of your own free will!" His words were words of reason, but they could hear the undertone of frustration sharpening them little by little.

"Nope!" Degory shouted, then whispered to Eurydice from the corner of his mouth, "do you have the rocket set up, yet?"

"I need to give it another twist or two," she fumbled with the dials lined up the rocket's body. No careful calibration, no set coordinates logged into the LWDT knobs. It was as likely to open a Jump Port halfway into a mountain. Or, it might open over the yellow clouds of the evening star. It might even open in the space between realities. "Your Imperial Majesty," she now called Emperor Norton.

"Why, yes Adeptus Priest." A smile spread across his face and he held up a hand, immediately silencing his grotesque army. "In what way may I be of service to yourself?"

"We've given some thought to your offer," she said, a slow smile spreading across her lips. "But I'm afraid we're going to have to decline." She cracked the rocket in half, mixing the fuel components and threw it high into the air.

The Emperor, Degory and his Minister watched the small tube arc against the sapphire sky. They were the only four able to understand the device's significance. At the peak of its ascent, the rocket flared to life like the hot end of an arc welder. It shot into the sky with a puff of smoke trailing behind before disappearing from view.

A swirling, angry void crackling with purple electricity opened like an evil eye. Deep within, dark clouds of particles, the color of an evil bruise, swirled in a powerful vortex. Eyes and things like eyes glared out with hungry expectation and a thousand voices cried out for flesh and blood. Arms and tentacles, fingers, claws and unnamable appendages reached out, snatching beasts and Celebrants alike, dragging them shrieking into the sentient space.

The wind roared and rocks and dust mixed with desert bracken flung themselves into the eye of the storm. The Emperor's tall hat loosed itself from the crown of his head and spun end over end into the whirling madness. The ferocity of wrath in his eyes transcended human emotion as he lashed the screaming wind.

"It's time," Degory shouted to his Minister, who nodded, his face gray but set and grim. "Do you think you'll be ok?" This he yelled to Eurydice as she shielded her face with her broad cybernetic hand.

"I'll have to be," she yelled back through the tumult. "I wish," but she hesitated.

"Wish what?" Degory gripped her shoulder. His legs buckled and he felt himself losing his balance to the vortex.

"I wish you hadn't been so damn stupid!" She had to spit it out; her remaining eye felt hot and overburdened, "we don't have time for this! You found me, now go get what you need to get done finished or we've," but she couldn't finish, Degory interrupted her thought with a final kiss.

"Hey," he said, smiling. "I found you before the end at least." Before she could stop him, he grabbed his Minister's arm and raced to close the distance to the Emperor.

What happened next did not take long. Degory and his Minister collided hard with Norton. Their shoulders hit his chest. The sword fell from Norton's hand, tipped toward the ground, but pulled into the vortex before it hit the ground. Norton fell back one, two, three steps from the combined force of the two men. Those three steps were all it took to push him into the event horizon. He didn't even scream as he fell back, torn from the birthplace of humanity forever.

Degory and his minister followed, to Eurydice's dismay, due to the simple laws of motion and inertia. She could not have saved them even if they were bound with nanofiber cables and titanium handcuffs. The three shapes passed through the event horizon, snapping it shut in a powerful explosion of displaced air and rubble. Eurydice went cartwheeling into a crowd of celebrants.

Eurydice Priest landed hard on the desert hardpan and darkness washed over her. She did not wake up for a long time.

Chapter 22

Eurydice woke in a crumpled, sun parched heap. Her bruised and battered body ached, but nothing felt broken or ruptured. Her artificial arm lay shattered beneath her, twisted beyond use. She loosened the straps binding it to her shoulders and allowed it to collapse to the ground in a broken heap. Her artificial eye had gone blind, marring half her vision with static and a litany of error messages. Slipping the fingers from her remaining hand into her socket, she pulled it out and threw it aside.

She had no way of knowing how long she'd been unconscious. The hordes of the Wild Hunt dispersed, leaving behind the shattered bodies of their dead. The air glowed sandy yellow, blown dust and mist obscuring her view after about 20 feet or so. A Celebrant left behind to shamble without direction bumped into her. An enthralled war boar stood silent but for its internal rumbling, but it made no moves.

The second after they passed through the portal, the Emperor's influence upon the Wild Hunt broke. Each celebrent found themselves free to wander into the desert to pursue their own fates. While no record exists for any of them, most speculated they all wandered off for the sands to consume them. Weak minds whipped into the orgiastic frenzies of the Wild Hunt fell beyond sanity's tenuous grasp.

Eurydice found herself alone.

"Hey."

Eurydice spun around; she'd heard that voice before, but had no face to connect to it.

"There's no need to wear yourself out. I want you to sit and breathe."

The voice had a calming effect. It pretended to be her internal monologue. But as much as it felt like her own voice, it still felt foreign, a clandestine echo. Eurydice sat, her chin drooping to her chest. She felt so tired and another couple of minutes of sleep wouldn't hurt a thing.

"Nope!" Again, that voice yelled at her with her own voice. "Time for napping is over! It's time to start thinking about survival now!"

Who needed survival when sleep was right around the corner?

"There'll be plenty of time to sleep, hey!" Her eyes snapped open and she looked, but the hand that slapped her remained as invisible as the hot air. "It's time to get up and move! You can survive this, but you're going to have to put your cerebrum in my control for the immediate future!"

How Eurydice found her will to move had no logical source. For all she cared about, she could have sat in the dust and turned to jerky. Even so she found her body searching for water, tools and resources. By the same token it was her own free will, at the same time it didn't feel like it.

Shadows extended as the day wore on. Despite her broken body, she found herself in the middle of a stretch of cracked and broken pavement. She wore a broad brimmed hat and an old army surplus coat, as well as a heavy duffel slung over her shoulder. Three full canteens hung clipped to the duffel strap, though she had no idea where she could have scrounged a drop from that wasteland.

She felt someone snapping around her face as if to rouse her attention, but again there was nobody. "Alright, Eu," again it was her own voice, but she wasn't thinking in that vein. "Time to pull your head out of your ass and start walking," it said. "We need to get to the other side of those mountains." Invisible hands craned her face around to look at the jagged spires to the west. "But first we need to start marching north, got it?"

"Got it," she mumbled, "but, one question?"

Her internal monologue made an exasperated sigh, "Fine," it huffed, "what? Never mind that we're already well behind schedule and we need you in those foothills by dusk."

"Who are you?" Eurydice tried turning around, but the voice in her mind turned her feet in the direction it wanted her to go. "You feel so familiar." Her hand rose, bringing a canteen to her lips and cool water relieved her dehydrated throat.

She waited to hear the voice, but heard nothing. Visions and emotions that weren't hers spun through her mind. She could see herself, as if she were standing before herself, but it was different. Diffuse. It appeared as though a projection of herself cast itself onto drifts of mist, but the mist was her and she was the mist. She felt pain and fear, but also longing and a powerful desire to learn and create. She felt her body draw itself out long and thin before a long, thin tube sucked her in, depositing her...

Here, she heard and felt now.

"I still don't think I understand," she muttered to herself, but she knew. Even when they were together, Degory said little. He explained little about his secret projects. Everything about what she felt, heard and saw now had his fingerprints all over it. And he was gone. Any chance for a future, any chance for explanation disappeared into the jump portal with him.

She felt something in her mouth. Rummaging deep in the corner of her cheek and jaw with her tongue, she felt something small, round and hard. Degory had passed something to her before plunging into eternity with his minister and Emperor Norton. She found a small round tablet in the corner of her mouth and spat it into her remaining hand.

It only looked like a pill; it was small, circular and half red, half black. She knew right away what it was. In life, Degory was many things. Impetuous, vague, a little psychotic, but never suicidal if he didn't think of a way out of a problem.

"Keep that safe," the voice in Eurydice's head said. "You don't need that now, but once we get to where we're going, I can explain a few more things a little better. Then you can do with that Tabula Vivifica what you will." The voice paused. Then it said, "Wait until we're ready before you decide what to do with it. You have more than enough time now."

Eurydice took a deep breath and slipped the small red and black circle into a pocket. The sun hung high over the mountains and she braced herself, facing the northwest road. He had no depth perception and only one arm, but her path rose to meet her feet, one step at a time. The voice told her their destination was the western side of those imposing black slabs. She knew the rumors and stories of monsters by heart, but now she had the impression it wouldn't be so bad. No people, no monsters. Peace would be her only companion.

She tightened her duffel's strap and walked onto the highway. The Novum Imperium Romanum was behind her. Despite the aching in her muscles and bones, it felt right to go on a journey of her own for once in her life.

Chapter 23

Eurydice sat in the doorway of her little cabin overlooking the vast swath of the western ocean. Fragrant tendrils of herbal smoke rose from her small clay pipe. The sun hung low above the horizon, scarlet radiance dappling the blue water. It was midsummer with warm, breezy nights by the ocean, but could not remember how long her search took. Her trip from Orevada in the desert wastes through the maze of mountains took at least a month. She progressed north and west, but always walked and always sought.

She knew her destination was close when the slope graded downwards and massive evergreens towered high above. She made it her habit to camp by day and walk by night with cool evening breezes fresh across her face. The Wild Hunt scattered after that final explosive day. Not even a wild dog or carrion fowl ventured near her path. Despite the loss of her bionic arm, she still carried a salvaged handgun and a hunting knife.

Whoever started the rumors that monsters dwelt in the *Mons vetiti*[24] were either lying or misled. Even the densest parts of the range in the darkest hours of the night her march went unmolested. Some nights she imagined she saw the tiny pinprick of a campfire on a distant peak. If it was set by human hands then they were hands that preferred their solitude and she left them to their privacy. She had plenty of water before she reached the first of the mountain streams. She also had enough food. The signs of game animals reassured her. She wouldn't starve after she emptied her last tin.

She gazed out over the clearing she had established and looked with relish at her little garden. She had rows of edible plants next to her medical herb garden. She even planted a

---

[24] Forbidden mountains

couple of rows to make sure her pipe never went empty. A nearby spring burbled with clean, fresh water. She drew in some smoke and let it out in a slow stream; today had been a good day.

She still had no idea how she had built the cabin. She knew her passenger, her secondary inner monologue, responsible for everything and it had Degory's stink all over it. Every time she felt despair stab at her heart, her ego gave way to whatever it was that now possessed her. She felt no fear of it, for it felt too much like a part of herself to be anything but herself, but even so, it unnerved her. She often tried talking with it, but always it was her own voice coming back to her inside her own head.

Her cabin and garden were the two least subtle acts of help it performed. Then, it fell into the back of her mind. With only one arm and one eye, she did not feel confident about her prospects of survival.

Strangest of all, once she saw her cabin complete, she remembered all that had happened to make it work. Scratches and light bruises scored her limbs and her muscles cried out from the long days of hard work. She watched through the eyes of another, but at the same time she felt the rough stone and lumber under her own hands.

Still, the voice never came back to her, but she still felt its influence. She dreamed of long black tendrils, light as silk. They left her body and spread out along the coastline for thousands of miles. She was aware of every single animal between the ocean and the mountains, and even some in the mountains. She sensed the predatory creatures and hid when they strayed too close. Sometimes the tendrils turned them from her territory out of instinct. She also knew where the slow, fat prey hid, and her tendrils guided them to her favorite hunting spots. Her extended senses found edible plants and sources of freshwater. When she went fishing, the fish all but jumped into her baskets.

Time passed and she felt more confident about her survival. Those very same tendrils extended even further and located an unexpected treasure trove. While exploring the woods around her cabin, Eurydice found an abandoned military outpost. Overrun with thick vines and overgrowth, it still bore the official imperial insignia. She would have passed it by had she not sensed it was there. She hacked away at trees and vines as thick as her wrist with her machete. She found enough equipment to keep her busy for months.

Much of the scrap had decayed beyond use, but she still found what she knew she could use. She no longer had to worry about the millions of ungrateful citizens of the city-state. This was her home to dwell and defend as she saw fit.

She soon had enough parts to build herself a new arm. Time was not so kind to the leftover optical equipment in the outpost and she had to scrap most of the technology. She would have to make do with an eye patch until she could do some more exploring, but there was enough time for that.

She used her free time to build her new arm right. This one was more refined than the one she had built in that filthy garage. It was stronger, flexible and she was able to scale it better to her body size. She admired the detail she put into her new hand. She made a fist, flexing the phalanges, delighted she didn't feel like a fiddler crab.

She took another puff from her pipe and enjoyed the red glowing ember burning deep in the bowl. She enjoyed the smell and flavor of the smoke and blew it out, watching its lazy rise in the warm summer air.

She reached into a pocket and fished the small tablet Degory passed to her during their final kiss. She looked at it. It was small, round and smooth, no larger than a head pill available at any chemist, legal or underground. The pill had a shiny, glassy coating over a red and black interior.

It was Degory's Tabula Vivifica, one of his more elaborate projects from their time together. In a way it was the perfect insurance policy. It was like a seed; she had to plant it in some soil and water it. Over the next few weeks, it would draw mass and nutrients from the soil forming a perfect copy of himself. Once the body reincarnated, the Tabula's energy would kickstart his heart and reboot his mind and memory. It wasn't a perfect system. She would have to remind him that he had died, but he had gotten better. It wasn't perfect, but it was still better than cloning.

She turned the little pill over in her hand and slipped it back into her pocket. The sun dipped below the horizon on the western sea now and she finished her pipe. She tapped the ashy contents out on her bootheel and stood, wincing as her joints popped. She would have plenty of time to plant the pill and bring Degory back, but for now she was ready for sleep. In another week, or month, when she was ready to end her solitude she would bring Degory back. They could even enjoy her cabin by the ocean together, but for now all was quiet.

And she enjoyed the quiet.

Omnia mutantur, nihil interit[25].

---

[25] Everything changes, nothing disappears.

About the Author

Adam Schubert is a lifelong resident of Wisconsin with a degree in Journalism from the University of Wisconsin, Milwaukee. He currently lives outside of Madison, where he spends time with his son, Ollie and partner, Lizz. His favorite authors are Mark Z. Danielewski, Stephen King and Shel Silverstein.

Printed in the USA
CPSIA information can be obtained
at www.ICGtesting.com
CBHW020155301124
18173CB00042B/353